Throughout

The

Ages

By:

Ryan Johnson

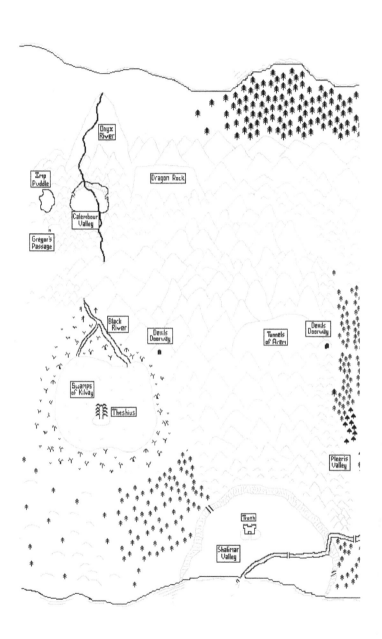

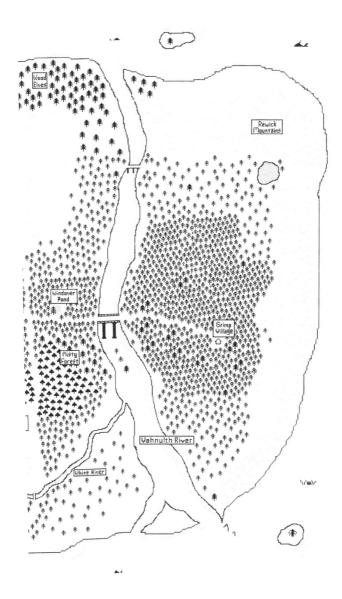

The Pasts End

ISBN: 978-1-7375030-0-2

DEDICATION

I want to thank my family for helping me on this journey.
It took nearly 25 years to complete this short novel and I
never could have accomplished that feat if it wasn't for
their support and encouragement. This book is for them!

ACKNOWLEDGMENTS

I would like to thank Rachel Gauthier for painstakingly
reading over my novel and correcting the multitude of
editorial errors. Also, Alexia Johnson for her artistic work
on the cover. Finally, I want to thank everyone who
helped push me to finish the work I started so many years
ago!

CONTENTS

Chapter 1

The Pasts End

Long, long ago, long before man was able to rule the skies, long before he sailed his ships in hope of finding passage to the farthest realms. It was a more medieval age, back when the master of the sword could declare his own law, and the lord of the steed could breach any terrain. Back when the most knowledgeable and skilled of all blacksmiths could forge weapons of such amazing powers, along with hidden magic abilities, that could give the strongest of wielders an uncanny advantage.

It was an age when great mages roamed the hillside, and the simple wave of their hand could make the grounds shake, or speaking an incantation could create a mighty tempest. It was a time when dragons roamed the endless skies and the forests housed the clever elf. It was an age when legend was truth, myth was a recollection of the tales of old, and an adventure was just a step away. This was the *Age of Magic*.

There were many creatures huddled together at the base of a great mountain. Some were short, heavier set, and covered head to toe with hair. Others were clad in deep shades of green to help them hide amongst the forest, and some also of many sizes were covered in a flowing cloak to hide their appearance, these were the mighty wizards.

There was a great battle that had taken place, the final of a long and gruesome war. Those that remained alive made up a small handful compared to the many dead bodies that scattered the ground. The trees had been burned, all vegetation was stomped dead in the ground, and the rocky foothills were soaked in a variety of colored blood spills of the deceased. What was left of a once beautiful countryside was now utterly destroyed by the most violent battle the world had ever seen.

This war, like all others, was a struggle for power. The mightiest of all dragons, and ruler of his kind, gathered numerous creatures of which he bribed with the promise of power and wealth to fight for his cause. He, the red dragon, recruited the goblins, orcs, trolls and other creatures of the depth that found joy in death and destruction. As the war grew, so did the vastness of the dragons' army, and destruction inevitably followed.

But this had now all ended. Both great armies attempted to lead the other into a trap, causing all reserves for both sides to surround the other creating a confusion of bloodshed. Death came from any and every angle as everyone from each side had to attempt to win the war on their own.

The battle had turned in favor of the mighty dragon and his forces, and those opposing him were beginning to lose hope. Then in the gloom and darkness of the battle, five cloaked figures appeared, each of a distinctly different race. These five summoned all their magic together and pit it against the mighty red dragon, in an attempt to end this war by destroying its source. Although the great red dragon was more powerful than even these five mages together, he was too confident in his powers and his cause to believe that these insignificant mortals could ever defeat him. This was the red dragon's downfall.

Now the only remains of this great tyrant is the stone carcass of which the wizards entrapped him in. These wizards knew that they, although very powerful themselves, were no match against the dragon. So, instead of attacking him with their powers as the dragon anticipated, they created a binding spell around him trapping him in the same rock that he once called his home.

A great reconstruction was now to begin, as the many different species returned to their families and the land they called home. The Great War was to never to be forgotten, and to always be a reminder to the people of every race and culture, so that this evil deed would never again bestow the land. Thus, was the end of the Age of Magic.

Chapter 2

The Village Elder

Far away from the planet we know and love, hidden in the deepest reaches of the universe rests a small planet known as Kureas. Kureas in most aspects is much like the earth was prior to its modernization. On its surface, Kureas is covered with crystal clear lakes, numerous trees and as many species as one could imagine. However, hidden below this serene exterior lies another world, a world cloaked in darkness and home to the foulest of creatures. These two territories provide a dreadfully distinct equilibrium between the good and evil of the planet.

The upper portion of this planet is known as Trubanius, yet more often referred to as the Lands Above. It is on this plane that the elves, grimps, colivien, dwarves, and all the other creatures of the forest reside, and also where our story begins. Scattered throughout the world of Trubanius are portals leading to Broudiun, which is more frequently noted as the Dark Realm, and the home of the orcs, goblins, trolls, the wicked strews, dredgee, shuliyts, and all the other sinister and malevolent creatures that lurk in the shadows. Fortunately for all those who call the Lands Above their home, each and every portal leading to the Dark Realm had been sealed after the demise of the great red dragon. Thus, it was a time of peace for Trubanius, as all who would rob the Lands Above of its glory were sealed away in the darkness.

It was a warm spring morning on Trubanius as the sun had just begun to peak over the treetops melting the remnants of the last snowfall of the winter. The birds began to whistle a beautiful song that wisped throughout the trees as the animals of the forest gradually became visible through the tree line and began drinking from a small pond. In what had once been a clearing in a great forest, a small community of sturdy little houses had been erected. These cozy little homes, which were built partly into the ground and partly out of the great stowl trees, were the dwelling places of grimps.

Now the grimp is a rather simple creature, yet at the same time so indefinite that a passing traveler could never situate them into a sentence. They are, oddly enough, closest in relation to the dwarves, however in their actions there could hardly be a creature they could have less in common with, other than maybe the creatures of the Dark Realm. The dwarves were burly miners and could prove very fierce and deadly opponents, whereas the grimps were mostly farmers and quite weak in comparison to their relatives. However, this was not always so. Long ago the grimps had been a very powerful race, using magic as their ally they were a key component in the destruction of the red dragon. Unfortunately, as the need for protection faded, along with it faded the mystical abilities of the grimps, and now only one could still master the magical arts.

As this new and gorgeous day begins, a young grimp known as Darius opens the door to his house and begins to venture down the now busy street.

Today is a very special day for the grimps, as it not only celebrates their New Year, but also three hundred glorious and peaceful years since The Great War. The grimp houses have all been decorated with an array of diversely colored streamers and lights, which had become a New Year's tradition. It was also customary for the house symbol, an enchanted or mystical creature from grimp lore, to be hung over the front door in honor of the history and greatness of the family name.

Now Darius, who is anxiously awaiting the

festivities to take place in the afternoon, begins walking down a dirt road admiring the many unique decorations and emblems hanging over each of the houses.

"Darius!" came a familiar voice.

Darius had just noticed his best friend Tristin, who had been chasing after him down the street. Now Tristin and Darius had been friends longer than either one of them could remember and were rarely seen apart, which was always a rare and pleasant site to the other grimps of the village considering these two were always getting into mischief. "Hold on Darius I have to talk to you."

A somewhat surprised Darius quickly responds, "I thought we were supposed to meet by the Great Oak, what are you doing over here?"

"Darius," Tristin quickly pulled him close and lowered his voice, somewhat hesitant to continue. "I don't really know how to tell you this but, umm, Heretius told me that the second I saw you this morning I was to send you over to his house immediately, and alone!"

"What!" Darius took a step back, waiting for Tristin to tell him it was only a joke, but a solemn, serious look remained on Tristin's face. Darius began taking short, panting breaths as a sudden fear sunk in. "Why? Am I in trouble? What did I do? Why Heretius?"

"Sorry Darius, he wouldn't tell me, whatever it is you did it must have been pretty bad if you have to see him. What a horrible thing to happen, especially today!"

Everything started to become hazy for Darius as he sank into a void of despair. Tristin's voice faded out of Darius' mind as he began slowly and unconsciously walking towards the home of Heretius.

Now Heretius, the oldest and most respected among the grimps is getting along in years and is the only grimp still able to control the powers of magic. Although Heretius is very powerful, there is no indication by his appearance that he would be of any threat, even to the weakest of creatures. If one were to see him walking along the forest paths the last feeling that would overtake them would be that of fear.

Heretius slowly rose from the comfort of his chair, and leisurely made his way to the kitchen, which was a sight in and of itself. At first glance, Heretius' kitchen appeared to consist of nothing more than a table surrounded by four chairs and four plain walls, which looked to have the color and texture of a living tree. Slowly Heretius makes his way toward his kitchen and reaches toward the empty wall. As if with magic a slight seam in the wood becomes visible and a door opens. Meticulously, he reaches into the cupboard and begins pulling out numerous oddly shaped containers and places them on a counter that also becomes suddenly visible beneath the cupboard. Then, as simply as it had appeared, Heretius closes the door and it blends back into the wall as if there had never been a cupboard there. After pulling out a large wooden spoon from a drawer hidden with equal indistinctiveness into the wall, he then sits down on his favorite chair to eat. However, just as Heretius raises the first spoonful of some sort of herbal soup to his mouth, there is a soft knock on his front door.

Heretius, seeming to barely have the strength to yell, calls out in a soft yet strong voice, "come on in Darius, the door is open."

The door slowly creaks open as Darius, full of questions, curiosity, and mostly fear walks into the cozy little home and quickly blurts out an apology, now worrying more than ever why the most respected and powerful of grimps would want to talk to him. "I'm so sorry Mr. Heretius sir, I promise it will never happen again!"

Without raising his eyes from the spoonful of soup Heretius speaks out, "I've been waiting all morning for you Darius, you young grimps waste too much of your morning sleeping so late. Please come over here."

The color was flushed out of Darius' face, his hands were shaking uncontrollably, and his chest hurt with every breath. Darius walked over to the side of Heretius' chair, held his chest high, and forced back the fear-induced tears.

"Young Darius," Heretius for the first time lifts his eyes to meet Darius'. Heretius paused, seemingly staring straight through Darius giving him the feeling that he was being interrogated. After a short while, what seemed like hours to the poor and confused Darius, Heretius slowly continued, "please, sit with me by the fire, I would like to tell you a tale."

A fragment of color had returned to Darius' face as the fear in his eyes was quickly replaced by a storm of curiosity. Darius' was beginning to feel sick. Was he in trouble, and what reason would Heretius have for speaking to him that anyone else in the village could not have simply told him? More and more questions began swarming into Darius' head as a short-lived fear turned into a petrifying terror. What could Darius have done that was so horrible, that he had to be sent to the elder for punishment?

"I'm not, err, I mean I didn't," more and more

questions began swarming in his head as he tried not to cast his gaze from Heretius without looking into his eyes. Darius was gradually becoming impatient, wishing to simply get this over with and adhere to his punishment.

"Darius", Heretius stopped for a moment trying to find the best way to tell the young grimp his important news, and then started to speak again. "Darius, what I have to tell you may be hard for you to understand, but you must listen to me and most of all trust me."

"Heretius, it wasn't me! I mean it wasn't on purpose." Tears began to build up in Darius' eyes as he did his best to apologize for whatever it was he undoubtedly did.

"DARIUS, please stop and simply listen!" Heretius' voice rose up to quell the apologetic murmurings of Darius. He then softly continued. "Now as I mentioned, I need to tell you a story. Many years ago, there was a time which was known as the Age of Magic. All Grimps, even those your age, were taught the secret of magic. But as the year's past, along with it the need, the grimps no longer saw a purpose for magic, and it was most unfortunately forgotten."

"But Heretius," Darius was now beginning to

realize that he didn't have the faintest idea what was going on, "you've told this story to me and my friends many times, why are you telling me again?" Darius still couldn't bring his eyes up to meet Heretius's. "So, am I in trouble or not?"

A hint of a smile flashed across Heretius' face before he continued with his lecture. "No Darius, you are not in trouble, unless you would like to take this time to confess any wrongdoings?" Heretius gave Darius a short moment before continuing, "now if you would do a very old grimp a favor and kindly keep your mouth shut."

A large sigh of relief flushed out of Darius, as he quickly cleared his throat trying to cover it up.

Pretending not to notice, Heretius continued. "There is much more to the story than those simple facts. If not, I wouldn't have called you to my home!" Heretius shifted slightly in his chair to get more comfortable and continued. "A long time ago, when I was a very young child we grimps were constantly in battle with the red dragon and his followers. This battle had been going on before my great-grandparents were alive. The great dragon was twisted with evil and wanted nothing less than to control this world and anything he might have encountered. Yet, not all the dragons were evil, there were a few that saw no purpose for fighting and were great allies with us. Without them, we would surely have been quickly overpowered and the red dragon would have destroyed us all.

On one very dreary day, as the sun had become hidden behind the smog of dragon fire and burning foliage, we were pitted in the worst battle that war had ever seen. The greatest wizards of my time had conjured up a plan and attempted to lead him and his clan into a trap. It was a long battle and many had died with the hope that we would once again regain our freedom. When the smoke had finally cleared, along with it ended another of the agonizing battles, and this time we had prevailed. Nevertheless, we knew if we didn't do something about our foes then and there, they would have regrouped, and this seemingly endless war would continue on. So, we gathered those strongest in magic and combined our powers to create a type of force field, trapping the red dragon and his strongest followers within a stone tomb. And to this day, our magic seal has held and there they remain prisoners. But as we ensnared him, the great dragon swore that someday he would get revenge on us. He promised that one day, when we have grown weak and forgotten our magic, he would break free and destroy us all!"

"But Heretius, I still don't see what this has to do with me?" Although the fear of punishment had left Darius he was still greatly puzzled by Heretius' story.

"Darius, as you know I am the only grimp left in this village that has the ability to control the powers of magic. I have lived a very long life and I have watched as each new generation enters this world and casts aside their heritage. I have been keeping an eye on you since your birth Darius. You see, you have the potential to gain the same powers as I, and you must learn to control it. For if I pass on and there is no one to take my place, the red dragon will surely break free and there will be no hope for any of us!"

A glow of nervousness and excitement quickly replaced the confusion that plagued Darius. "So, are you going to teach me how to do magic!?" Darius was elated, he couldn't wait to learn some cool tricks and then run off and show Tristin and dazzle the other grimps of the village.

Heretius lowered his head, almost ashamed of his age, and then speaks. "Young Darius, I'm afraid that I am too old and weak to teach you properly. When I was your age, many years ago, we had a tradition. Before a grimp could truly learn our sacred arts, they would first be sent off on a quest. This Darius, is the same task I place before you. I would ask that journey to Theshius, for she is the only one left who might still own the books of magic which you will need. Once you have learned the ways of your ancestors you must travel to the great Dragon Rock, add your own seal to the stone, so that our people can continue to live in peace."

"But Heretius! How can I possibly travel all the way to Theshius, she lives on the other side of the world! And, I'm not a fighter I wouldn't make it. I've never gone anywhere on my own. And my parents!"

"Slow down Darius, I realize how hard this must be on you, and for that reason I would do no more than simply ask that you contemplate your options. Also, know this, although your task may be of the utmost importance, you will not be alone. Before this is over, every grimp in the village will play a role in protecting our world and way of life, along with many other creatures of the forest that are unknown to you. I fear we may have already waited far too long to reunite the creatures of Trubanius, so I am forced to ask you to make your decision today. There is no greater task that I could ask of you so, I will understand and respect whatever decision you come to."

There was a long pause as both Darius and Heretius let their gazes fall to the floor, deep in thought. Darius couldn't keep his arms from shaking as a familiar feeling of sickness once again overtook him. Slowly he raised his head as if he were preparing to leave Heretius' home as he tightly closed his eyes and forced three words from his lips. "I will go."

Heretius nearly slipped from his chair in shock. He had by no means expected Darius to make a decision so quickly. There was a look of sadness in Heretius' eyes and a large smile on his face as he looked at Darius. "You never fail to surprise me Darius, and I don't know if you will ever fully know the importance of your decision. I will prepare a map for you that will lead you to the home of Theshius, which will be the first of many trials during your quest. But as for now, I want you to go into the village and prepare for your journey, enjoy the festivities, say your good-byes, get a long night's sleep, and then return first thing tomorrow. If you have any questions or concerns, I will do my best to help you."

A familiar glazed look once again plagued Darius' face as he slowly got up and walked out the door without saying a word. As he walked down the street, Darius watched as the other kids were playing games, unaware that these next few weeks could be their last.

Darius' unvoiced gaze was suddenly broken as a figure flashed across the corner of his eyes. It was the familiar sight of Tristin running towards him, inquiring about the conversation that took place at Heretius' home and wondering what horrible punishment was awaiting him.

Tristin waited till he was within a whispering distance before he confronted Darius so that the other grimps wouldn't overhear them. "So, tell me what happened! It couldn't have been that bad, I mean at least he didn't turn you into a goblin or something worse!"

"Well," Darius slowly brought his gaze up to meet Tristin's. "I think it might be worse."

"What could possibly be worse?" questioned Tristin, a little uneasily. If it hadn't been for the fact that Darius had just visited Heretius he would have thought nothing about the matter. However, anything regarding the village elder was very serious business.

"He, well, he told me that I that,,," muttered Darius as he slowly tightened his eyes, wishing to wake up and have the day start fresh, without Heretius and without his decision to leave the village.

After about ten minutes Darius had explained the whole situation to Tristin. With an empty stare, Darius waited for that special advice that could only be given by a best friend.

"Are you kidding!" screamed Tristin, not realizing how loud he let his voice grow. "That is one of the greatest things I've ever heard! How is it that you're so lucky?"

"What?" replied Darius, who had an equally loud and somewhat ringing shock in his voice. "What do you mean by lucky! Yeah, that's just great, lucky me, yippy, I get to go and die in the forest. Wow, and I thought today couldn't get any better with the festival, but wow was I wrong. Look out everybody, lucky grimp a'comin through!"

Tristin shook his head as he pushed Darius away from the street along with the prying ears of the grimps who began eavesdropping after the two had inadvertently raised their voices. "You know Darius, I think your kind of overdramatizing the whole situation. I mean how many times have we wished we could go on a great adventure into the forest? How often have we pretended we were great wizards like Heretius, and defeated a room full of trolls and goblins with the simple wave of a hand? You have been given the opportunity to follow your dreams and get out of this useless town. You get to see the world! And, what's better yet you, Darius, will return to us a great wizard and tell all the children your great tale. Then, every grimp in the town, heck probably the world will know the story of Darius the great wizard, and write stories about you for years to come."

"At least your optimistic!" Darius said with a roll of his eyes. "Yeah, maybe all that could happen, but I think you're forgetting one small, tiny, almost insignificant detail. It took the five most powerful wizards of the time, who had probably trained since, well, before they could walk, and all they could manage was to trap him in a rock! Now I have to travel to the ends of the world and learn how to add to a seal before the dragon can break free! And what happens if I'm not strong enough or quick enough? What happens if the dragon breaks out before I get there?! Maybe, yeah that's it, maybe I'll just waltz on up to the old dragon, and he'll think my pathetic powers are so funny that he'll laugh himself to death! That's it, that will be my plan of attack!"

"Well heck, at least you haven't lost your sense of humor," Tristin laughed. "If you want, I'll go with you. Maybe I have what it takes to do a little magic."

After taking a long deep breath, Darius tried to change the subject. "Why don't we go and see how the decorating for the big celebration is getting along. You know it may be quite sometime before the two of us are together again to pull some practical joke. At least then maybe I'll really have something I can be remembered by. But, first I have to go and tell my parents; I'm sure they're going to have plenty to say about this."

"Okay buddy, I'll meet you by the old oak tree in say, two hours?" replied Tristin as he ran off darting behind shrubs as if he were on some secret mission.

As Darius continued his walk home, he had an incessant feeling that every other grimp in the village knew what had happened with him while he was at Heretius', and their every stare pierced into him. After a short walk, Darius had reached the front door to his home and prepared himself for more of the worst.

"Oh, Darius!" cried out a rather surprised mother. "I wasn't expecting you to be home already, but since you are you might as well sit down and have some lunch." As she watched her son slowly make his way to the dinner table, her motherly instincts immediately kicked in. "Why is it that your home so early? Are you in trouble? All right young grimp, what did you do!"

Before Darius could begin to tell his mother what had happened, the front door flew open and another familiar face walked in. Darius' father, home from work for lunch, gave the two a quick smile and sat down at the table next to Darius in anticipation of food.

"Well, well, I suppose you're home just in time." Darius' mother had turned her attention back to him, her eyes drilling through him much the same as Heretius' had. "I believe your son has something he is going to tell us."

With that deeply recognizable look, Darius' father turned his attention toward his son, cradling his head with his hand waiting to hear what recent dilemma Darius had found himself in this time.

Taking a deep breath, and shutting his eyes as tightly as they could go, Darius began to tell his tale for the second time. As he furthered himself into the story, Darius' parents went through many stages of emotional feelings. First, they were angry, thinking this visit to Heretius had to do with him getting in trouble, much as Darius had thought. Secondly, disbelief overtook them by the oddity of his story. Thirdly, an annoyance sunk in as they listened to this wholly farfetched fairy-tale. And finally, a great fear overtook them, as they both realized that the only way Darius could have found out many of the details of his story would have been if he had truly visited the town elder.

After a long silence, an unavoidably and

excruciatingly long lunch was filled with a great deal of answerless questions. As more and more problems, questions, and concerns filled the room, with answers met only in the form of other questions, Darius' parents decided that they must go and see the village elder themselves to sort this whole matter out.

Darius suddenly found himself at an empty table while a returning sickness once again overtook him. A tear had found its way down Darius cheek and landed on the dinner table. Little by little, Darius' head fell into his folded arms on the table as a storm of emotions began to flood out. While sitting all alone at the table, the only comprehensible words that escaped Darius' lips were,

"Why me?"

Chapter 3

The Festival

Darius slowly raised his head, as the tears still poured down his face. Rubbing his eyes, trying to bring the contents of the room back into focus, his eyes fell upon the clock hanging on the kitchen wall. "Oh no, I'm going to be late! Best not worry about tomorrow while there are festivities to be celebrated today."

With that, Darius quickly cleared his eyes of any signs of tears, and rushed out the door.

Tristin was beginning to grow rather impatient as he glanced yet again to his pocket watch, wondering what could be taking his friend so long, even though deep down he knew what Darius had to be going through. Yet, just as Tristin had given up hope that Darius would make it to the Great Oak, there came that recognizable little figure racing down the street.

"Ha! Glad you decided to show up," Tristin declared pretending to be slightly upset with Darius' untimely arrival.

"Oh, come on now," Darius then lowered his voice so that the other grimps standing around couldn't hear him, "Is everything ready for tonight?"

The serious look on Tristin's face was immediately replaced by an oversized smile. "Darius, have I yet to let you down? Now let's go or we'll miss the start of the party!"

With that, the two quickly dashed off towards the village square.

The census could always be taken at the New Year's festival, since there was never a grimp that didn't attend. Although it wasn't necessary, as there also wasn't a grimp in his working years that didn't know the names of every other grimp in the village.

The village square was beautifully decorated, with numerous and vibrant colors encircling everything. Tents were set up everywhere, with all sorts of wonderful food and overpriced novelties.

It was now well past suppertime, as the sun had begun to fall behind the trees. The colorful lights suddenly burst to life as if it were by some magical incantation, and the band struck up a lively tune enticing many to dance. For a moment, Darius had forgotten all the perils that tomorrow would bring and was uplifted by the joyfulness of the town.

As the two were walking past the many small shops Darius heard his name being whispered out from the inside of a small enclosed tent. "Darius. Darius, come here please."

Tristin and Darius stared at each other and then back at the tent, then with a bit of hesitation the two stepped inside.

"Ah, it's you Heretius. You had me worried there for a bit." Darius sighed with some relief.

"I'm sorry to have pulled you from the feast, but there is something of great importance that I must give to you."

Darius turned towards Tristin with a suddenly large smile. Any gift given by the town elder was definitely something worth being pulled from the party for.

Heretius then turned towards Tristin, "My lad, this doesn't concern you." But before Tristin could voice his disapproval, Heretius continued. "However, since you would most undoubtedly hide yourself near the entrance and listen anyway, I will allow you to stay. Just try and stay out of the way."

Tristin gave a short nod and let that conversation die.

Heretius then turned his attention back towards Darius, casting Tristin from the discussion. "Now Darius, what I have to give you can neither be seen, nor felt. That is, until it is put to proper use then it will be both." Heretius had a sly grin, like a father who just told a joke that only he thought was funny.

At that Darius gave a shifted glace back towards Tristin, rolled his eyes, and took a seat next to Heretius preparing himself for another long lecture.

The grin faded from Heretius' face. Taking the hint, he decided to cut the talking short. "As I told you earlier Darius, I won't be the one to teach you any real magic for I'm too old to justly do so. Nevertheless, what I can do for you is help prepare you for the trials you will face ahead. I have decided to teach you a simple combustion spell, in the hope that once you have learned one spell the rest may come a little easier to you."

With that wonderful news, Darius quickly sat upright from his stool eager to learn his first spell.

"Now first off, you must know this," continued Heretius.

Tristin silently whispered to Darius, "okay, this part must be the lecture."

With a cold stare aimed toward Tristin, Heretius continued. "First of all, this may be one of the most important things you ever learn about the use of magic, and it is simply this. True magic lies within." With an outstretched arm, Heretius placed his finger over Darius' chest. "Knowing the words to say and not having the spark of magic within you can never produce true results. So, in other words, simply waving a stick in the air and reciting some verses you read in some book will not create magic."

"Oh, I guess that makes sense now. I only wish I had known that years ago." Tristin replied hitting himself on the side of the head.

Scratching his head curiously, in hopes to learn more, Darius asked, "What did you mean when you said, true magic lies within."

"Well, simply enough it's just that," explained Heretius. "To make magic work, and more importantly, work the way you want it to, you must first feel it inside yourself. For example, let's work with the combustion spell. In order to make a fire in this world, you must first imagine it in the one inside your head. Focus on that fire, concentrate on its attributes, and then, and only then, bring that fire out."

With that, Heretius closed his eyes for a few moments, almost as if he had fallen asleep. Very silently under his breath he muttered the word "fotia" and instantaneously, on the tip of his finger on his outstretched arm, a small blue flame jumped off onto a small stick on the ground, quickly consuming it.

"Wow! That's amazing," howled Tristin, once again drawing more attention to himself than he would have liked.

"Now, I think it would be wise for you to practice this awhile. I would like to know that you could handle a flame, however small it may be, so I know you will have what it takes once you reach Theshius." Heretius replied, as he gave Darius a quick wink.

"I believe I will leave you two alone for now. Seeing as you will not have my help once you leave this village, I would like to know that you can do this on your own in the future." With that Heretius left the tent, leaving Darius and Tristin to their task.

Darius and Tristin wasted no time after Heretius left. Both immediately closed their eyes in an attempt to master the art of magic. As the hours passed, both Darius and Tristin fought to ignore the gleeful sounds that constantly leaked into the tent from the festivities. Forcing their minds to remain clear and their thoughts focused fully on one single goal. Yet one thing seemed to be missing, the fire.

"Darius," whispered Tristin, letting his shoulders fall in defeat, yet finally learning to keep his voice down. "I can't do it. Do you think this was another test and Heretius just wanted to see how long he could keep us quiet?"

"You know, Tristin..." looking up and meeting Tristin's gaze, as his concentration was now broken. "I don't think magic is supposed to be easy. I mean, if learning magic didn't involve work, why would our grandparents have forgotten the art. Do you remember when you were learning to swim? You were ready to give up on that after about two minutes, and now you swim circles around me!"

"I suppose," sighed Tristin. "I guess I've just wanted to be able to do magic my whole life, I'm sort of impatient. I'm not even the one who is supposed to be able to do this stuff."

"True, although Heretius told me that once all the grimps could use magic, to an extent. So, we should both be able to learn this, but for now we had better practice some more." Darius lowered his head, closed his eyes, and returned to his magic-making lesson.

Meanwhile, back at the village square... The raucous festivities continued. Although it was late into the night, the festival had just hit its full swing. Half of the village was dancing a song of grimpish lore, while the others were partaking in the great feast. Grimp food and music has a way of healing the heart and strengthening the spirit, as even the parents of Darius had seemed to have forgotten their troubles as they joined in the celebration.

Now, all great things must eventually come to an end, even the illustrious feast of the grimps. However, not one grimp in the village expected anything so abrupt. While in the middle of a lively song, the grimp band came to an unexpected and grinding halt. Many of the grimps who at the time were dancing in the middle of the square, inadvertently dropped their partners while those eating let their food slip from their hands and splatter over the many other dishes on the table.

Afterward, a loud and sarcastic "Oh, now here's a big surprise!" was yelled out from somewhere in the crowd.

Everyone's attention was drawn towards the stage where the band was currently playing in response to the cloaked figure standing there. Heretius had always been known for his brilliant ability to gain the attention of large crowds whose individuals were all indulged in their own conversations. As quickly as the music stopped, all of the grimps realized what had just happened and a loud clatter of voices filled the village square, as each and every grimp voiced their disapproval in the pausing of their celebration.

"Silence!" The commanding voice of Heretius echoed through the village, filling every space and void with wonder. For the grimps, it was always with amazement to hear Heretius use the full capacity of his voice. A grimp who was as old and outwardly weak seeming, Heretius could have probably destroyed the whole village on his own, if he ever thought the need was there.

Once Heretius knew he had the full attention of the entire village, he began. "My fellow grimps, my companions and friends. I am so very sorry to have paused this great festival; unfortunately, a need for me to do so has arisen. I want each and every one of you to know of a certain situation that has arisen in our village, before the inevitable rumors find your ears." Heretius paused for a moment to regain his breath and composure, and also to keep the tension in the crowd high enough to ensure their full and utmost attention. With a deep breath, Heretius continued. "If you look around, you may notice that two of our younger acquaintances are not with us. One of these two young grimps must take an unfortunate yet necessary leave from our village. He will be departing from us early tomorrow morning and neither he nor I will know when he shall return. Now I would like to ask a favor of all of you, if you could please..."

But before Heretius could finish his sentence a loud scream of "FIRE!" was called out from amongst the crowd.

It appeared that while everyone had been distracted by Heretius' speech, one of the many bonfires had set a nearby tent ablaze. The village was in an immediate panic as many of the grimps scattered in search of water to quench the now roaring fire and prevent it from spreading. While simultaneously, many of the other grimps of the village were equally running around, yet without many positive results as irrational panic had taken hold of them.

Thankfully for the village, one of their associates had previously been a great wizard and was still a very decent one in his old age. And so Heretius silently rose his arms into the air and called forth a tempest, which curiously enough was concentrated purely on the now overgrown fire.

Within a few moments, the torrents of rain subsided. With it, the fire was now also gone leaving behind only the fragments of the now-demolished tent. In the center of the carnage were remnants of singed cloth and support poles of the tent, and they seemed to be moving! Slowly, two charred figures rose to find themselves standing in the center of a scorched ring, with the eyes of the entire village on them.

Most of the grimps seemed unsurprised to find out that Darius and Tristin were the cause of the fire. Without question, if it weren't for the unusual laughter coming from Heretius, the two would have undoubtedly found themselves in a mountain of trouble.

Heretius then continued to speak to the villagers in a strange comical tone, although with somewhat less attention from the crowd this time around. "My friends, I see you have figured out who had been missing from your festival! Darius, Tristin, please come and stand here next to me."

Both Tristin and Darius received many malicious stares as they made their way past the crowd and up the stage to Heretius side. A few grimps commented that maybe they would be better off letting both troublemakers leave the village. At the same time, many of the other grimps seemed to question why anyone would have to leave since all their needs were provided for, in one way or another, right here in the village.

As Darius took his place next to Heretius on the stage, Heretius whispered to him. "So, I see you've figured out how to cast some magic."

"Well," Darius replied with a grin, "I may have learned how to cast some magic, but I think I need some practice controlling it."

With a smile, Heretius turned his attention back to the crowd. "Yes, that young grimp that I spoke of earlier who would have to leave our presence is in fact, Darius. Yes, it is very unfortunate that he should have to leave us, and I regretfully cannot explain the reason why at this time. You must place some trust in me, but much, much more trust and faith must be placed upon Darius. Hopefully, in a short while, I will have more answers for your foreseeable questions, but for now you must all display some patience. Moreover, please do not burden our young friend here with questions of his task. He is to leave tomorrow and would be much better off if he could do so in peace and with your blessings.   Oh, and one last thing, don't be too hard on him due to the fire that he caused, when a young grimp is in the process of learning magic it may often have unpleasant results."

At that, the village square instantly erupted with the chatter and whispers at even the mere mention of magic. As magic had long died off from the world there had always been a strong following who opposed its use. For although there are many wonderful blessings that come with magic, so too was its curse. With great magic comes great power, and with that power very often follows greed. It was that greed that caused the great war centuries ago and that fear that caused magic's downfall. This fear of greed caused the elders from centuries ago to banish the study of magic among the races in hopes that a simpler way of life would create a safer way of existence. Now in the sheltered world of the grimps, only Heretius remained with the knowledge of this ancient art.

A large crowd had quickly developed around

both of Darius' parents, as a torrent of questions were being hurtled in their direction. Yet, before any of these questions could be answered, Heretius delivered a bone-piercing stare that struck both of Darius' parents. It was a clear message that not a word was to be said without his consultation.

Darius spent the rest of the evening sitting at the banquet table next to Heretius, watching him perform various magic tricks and receiving advice on the correct ways to achieve the same results.

The party lasted long into the morning hours, but together Heretius and his parents had convinced Darius to go home and get some sleep. A long day was to await our young hero, as the first day of a long and grueling adventure was to begin.

Chapter 4

And so the Quest Begins

All that Darius could remember of his leaving the village was a number of people he had never met before hugging him, and wishing him a safe and happy journey.

"If only I could be back in the village," Darius thought, as his breaths were coming in short gasps, and his legs were beginning to feel like some sort of jelly. Darius hadn't even made a half a day's journey from his house before running into his first trial. A pack of hungry and ravenous blue wolves had picked up his trail.

His heart was beating faster and faster, never in all his life had he run as fast or as long. He let the backpack he had been carrying fall from his shoulders, forcing his weary body to push on. Darius began dodging around the trees of the forest as he scampered deeper and deeper within, straying farther and farther from the path.

The wolves shorten their gap on Darius and were now close enough to him that he could hear each and every breath they took as they strove for the kill. He could feel the cold hand of death pulling at him, coaxing him to give up and let the wolves take him. The light of the forest was beginning to fade and the trees began to move closer and closer together, as if they too were against Darius, trying to prevent his escape from his enemies.

The howl of the wolves was increasing in ferocity and deafening in sound, as their numbers grew poor Darius' lead began to dwindle. The wolves were now so close Darius could feel the warmth of their breath on his heels. The forest itself seemed to be against him as the branches began to grow so thick that they become nearly impenetrable and Darius had to shield his face as he pushed through them.

A sharp and piercing pain struck Darius' heel. Drops of blood began to roll down the chin of the nearest wolf as it has managed to sink one of its deadly fangs into him. Fighting through the pain Darius continued on, pushing himself farther and farther into the forest. Suddenly, as if the woods themselves had completely turned on Darius, a small branch tripped him up. In seconds dozens of wolves were upon him. Fighting with every ounce of strength he had left, Darius punched and kicked, refusing to let the wolves take him, he must carry on and complete his mission.

"OW! Hey, wake up before you break something." Cried, Darius' father, clutching his hand over his chest.

Darius opened his eyes and hurtled his body across the room. After a few short moments the realization of what was happening hits Darius and unconsciously he let his body fall to the floor. "Oh, thank goodness! It was only a dream."

"Well if you're going to be fighting like that, I'm going to start to feel sorry for anything in the forest that gets in your way." Laughed Darius' father as he began walking out of the room. "Get dressed. Then come in the kitchen and have some breakfast with your mother and I."

Both Darius and his parents were uncomfortable eating their breakfast. All three knew that this could very well be their last meal together, and no one could think of anything appropriate to talk about while they ate.

The morning seemed to pass by far more quickly than either Darius or his parents would have hoped. However, the time soon came for the three to make their way towards the home of Heretius. Darius' mother had filled a pack for him containing all the necessary items one might need for a trip away from home, such as a change of clothes for the varying climates, along with food and bottled water.

After a brief look around the home he grew up in, Darius slowly grabbed his pack and headed out the door with his parents. As they made their way out the front door the three grimps were amazed to see that the whole village had lined the street to say their farewells to Darius. Although, it appeared that the villagers had simply never ended their celebration from the night before.

Darius' father leaned over and whispered to both Darius and his mother. "Do you suppose they managed to coax some information out of Heretius? I don't see why else they would all be so concerned with Darius leaving to perform what Heretius called a small task."

Darius and his mother were both puzzled by the situation, and simply shrugged at the father's questions.

It was a very solemn march to the home of

Heretius. Even though the whole village followed behind Darius and his parents, not a word was said other than the occasional muffled whispers of the curious villagers.

Eventually, they had reached Heretius's front door. Rather hesitantly, Darius knocked. In what seemed like an instant, Heretius had opened the door, almost as if he had been sitting there waiting for Darius to arrive.

After taking a quick look around at the gathered villagers, Heretius then spoke. "I would like to speak to Darius alone for a while, if I may." Then turning to meet the gaze of Darius, he continued in a quieter tone. "Come along Darius, and shut the door behind you."

Complying with Heretius's instructions, Darius quickly follows behind and into the home of Heretius. The powers that were hidden within Heretius did not in the least bit resemble his home. Heretius had all the basics and nothing more, or it seemed to Darius. Everything was very dull and set away in its own place, and there were no magically enchanted artifacts lying about, or anything that might tell of Heretius' true self.

A small smile found its way onto Heretius' face as he speaks to Darius in the confines of his home. "Darius my poor grimp, it's truly a shame that your parting from this village be looked upon as a curse. Back when I was younger, much like you, when a grimp was to leave the village he or she was the envy of all the youth. For a grimps leaving meant that they were about to leave their childhood behind, and when they returned from their quest, they became known as powerful and accomplished wizards. And, in the same way, your leaving will be much like the trials that I faced. Only, I pray the roads are a much safer way to travel than in my youth."

"Is this supposed to cheer me up?" Darius blurted out before he could catch himself. In the end, there was a very different set of circumstances separating Heretius's journey as a youth and Darius'.

Heretius, taking no notice of Darius' response, slowly walked over to a large wooden trunk hidden in the corner of the room. After a short while, and a great deal of rummaging through his old trunk, Heretius gives out a short cry of joy. "Haha, there you are you old rascal." Heretius then quickly walked back over to Darius and sits down next to him. "As I told you earlier, this isn't going to be easy. On the contrary, this could just likely be one of the most impossible tasks anyone could ever ask you to perform. If all goes well, you will have only to travel through the Misty Forest, and cross the Morbid

Swamps to reach the home of Theshius. From there you must travel to Dragon Rock, in hopes of reinforcing the bindings on the dragon and his clan before they have the chance to free themselves of their prison and revive their army of darkness."

Darius couldn't speak. He knew that this was going to be a long and hard journey, but everything that Heretius was telling him seemed to be adding more and more weight to his burden.

"Come now Darius, lift your spirits some." Heretius had taken notice of Darius, who was making himself sick with fear. "Although you may think you're all alone in your quest, and all the creatures of the world want nothing more than to destroy you, just remember this, all the living things in this world that can recall the Great War, will never forget its consequences. All those living things that don't have a memory of the Great War yet have still tasted the joys of freedom and peace, make sure allies. The world itself, the trees, plants, rocks, and even the dirt in the ground are all part of a cycle that is life, and that make up all living things along with their own magical abilities. So as long as these all exist, you will never be alone. This world doesn't want to be overtaken by evil any more than you or me. So, as long as there is hope, as long as you carry as your ally something as great as the will to carry on, you will never be alone, and your quest to destroy evil will continue.

I wish there was more that I could do for you, or that you might stay with your friends and family and never have knowledge of orcs, goblins, or dragons. Unfortunately, wishing and hoping can't change the past, nor can it change the trials that the present unfolds before us. All we can do now is trust our fate in you Darius, that you might find something in yourself so great that even you can't fathom your abilities. Yet, before you leave the sanctity of the village, I would like to give you a gift that may prove very useful in your upcoming trials."

Heretius then lifted from his lap a pile of tattered rags that he retrieved from his old trunk. Slowly Heretius peeled away at the pile until a long dagger appeared. "This dagger was once my most trustworthy companion, in a time when the fear you face now was all around us. Although you will soon carry with you a power far greater than any steel, this may help you in times when magic will not. I also want you to have this."

Heretius then digs into another pile of rags and pulls out a small medallion. "This, Darius, is the Talisman of Odigia, or more commonly called the Talisman of Direction. Though your path may be uncertain to you, this talisman will help to guide you.

It contains magic far greater and older than even the greatest trees of the forest. With this, you might find the right path to defeating your enemies and possibly even restoring peace to Trubanius. And also, as I may have mentioned earlier, I have for you a map. This is the same map that once guided me through the great forests and will now be your direction and the only truth you may likely find in the world. For although trees may grow to alter your path and rivers may ebb and flow to alter their course the major landmarks on your journey remain unaltered throughout the recent age. Now, it is time for you to begin your journey from our village. I know your head must be swarming with questions, but these can only be answered with time, and a little luck.

Lastly Darius, heed this warning, don't stray from the path no matter what! For once you lose your way, the forest can become a confusing maze. Also, beware of the forest itself, for although there is still much good in the world, there are also many dangers lurking around every bush. I can't do any more to prepare you for what you will encounter, besides telling you to trust your thoughts, only when you stray from what you know is to be right will you fail. And remember, this village and possibly the world are relying on you. Once you find Theshius you must lock away the Great Dragon. If you lose your way, try and find the White River, it will lead you back to the village of Troth, from there you can take the path north to Theshius. Now be off young hero, and God's speed be with you."

With a deep breath, and a will of determination, Darius stood up and made his way out the front door. "Goodbye Heretius, I will return to you."

"Goodbye Darius", Heretius then whispers, "I pray you return victorious, for the fate of the world rests on you young one."

Without another word, Darius takes up his belongings, gives his parents a kiss and hug goodbye, says his farewells to his friends and the grimps of the village, and walks down to the edge of the forest where the dirt road begins. And with that step he begins his journey into the forest, not knowing what real dangers lay ahead.

Chapter 5

The Berkun Tree

As Darius' mother watched the shadow of her only child pass away into the uncertainties of the forest, tears of pain poured from her face as she tried to find some comfort in the arms of her husband. The villagers watched in awe, still not having any real clue as to the dangers that not only Darius would face, but also the most certain and cruel fate that they too would face if Darius were to fail.

Hidden in the back of the crowd, a small grimp let a single tear fall in farewell to a lifelong friend. Tristin watched as his best friend disappeared into the forest, leaving his home and giving up all he knew and loved. Tristin had then realized how great a friend Darius had been as he softly whispered to himself, "Farewell my friend, and don't worry, you won't be alone for long."

After walking far enough into the forest so that he was completely hidden amongst the trees, Darius paused. "So, this is it, this is the beginning." Darius then turned his attention to the large redwood trees. "Well, guess it's just going to be you and me, so I hope you have some decent fireside stories or this is going to be one long and lonely trip."

The forest was very beautiful and filled with the rejuvenating life that spring always brings. The many trees were all bursting with brilliantly colored blossoms, as the sunlight penetrated through the branches illuminating the dirt road. In an age long past this same road had once been part of a great system of highways linking the warriors of the Great War together. These days the road, seldom traveled by peddlers, was mostly overgrown and little resembled what anyone would call a road.

Now although the forest as a whole was the home to many malicious creatures, it was broken up into a few segments. Just over a day's walk from the village was a large river known as the Vahnulth River. This river acted as a natural barrier keeping all the foul creatures of the forest on the West side, while providing protection for the grimp village on the East.

The Berkun Tree

None of the grimp folk, other than Heretius who seemed to know just about everything (or so the grimps thought), knew why the creatures of the forest never crossed the Vahnulth. For although the great Vahnulth was deep and its water torrent, a strong and sturdy bridge spanned the gap between the two shores.

It was a shame that anyone had ever told Darius about the many dangerous creatures in the forest, for although it may have better prepared him for the roads ahead, it greatly ruined the beauty and pleasantness that lay to the east of the river.

Luckily enough for Darius, the long walk between the village and the bridge of Vahnulth was enough to let him somewhat ease his way into this journey that was forced upon him.

After about an hour's walk, Darius began to feel a large burden be lifted off his shoulders. He may be on his path to certain doom, but at least he no longer had the question-filled eyes of a village full of grimps constantly upon him. With that, Darius then began to whistle a lively grimp song as he reached into his pack in search of the map that Heretius had given to him, prior to his leaving the village.

As Darius began surveying the map, the lively tune faded from his lips and a familiar weight found its way back upon his spirits, smoldering his confidence and hopes of an easy journey. Despite the promising simplicity that the beginning of his quest presented, everything that followed looked as though it would be Darius' demise. Nearly another day's march past the bridge of Vahnulth was a small pond named Windover pond, which marked the path's decision to split. The path broke into three directions. Firstly, there was a northerly route, which would lead him over the Cliffs of Shemod, cross the Black River, and then through the Swamps of Kilvay. The second route continued west and was the shortest of the three paths. If Darius were to take this course he would have to travel through Death's Doorway, the long Tunnel of Arem, which was carved by Darius' Dwarfish relatives, connecting the two sides of the path under the Shemod mountain range. After emerging from the tunnel, Darius would then have to enter the Swamps to find the home of Theshius. And the third and final course that Darius could take would lead him south, and appeared as if it would be the least treacherous approach. Although the southern path was the longest of the three paths, he would only have to descend into the valley of Shalimar, cross over the White River, climb up a cliff out of the valley, and then it would be a short walk to the swamps, where again he would have to locate the home the Theshius.

Darius didn't know what to do. Almost immediately he ruled out the Cliffs of Shemod, so it would come down to a speedy journey to Theshius through the caves of Arem, or an easier, much longer road south. Fortunately, Darius would still have all the following day and the beginning of the next to decide the direction his journey would take, so he decided to put the map away and enjoy the forest while he still could.

Although the day was a simple and carefree hike for Darius, Heretius's day was proving to be much more troublesome. The grimps of the village were much more persistent than Heretius had ever given them credit for. It was only noon, and Darius had just left them five hours prior, and the grimps were already relentlessly attacking Heretius along with Darius' parents for information.

Tristin watched as Heretius tried to calm down the crowd of villagers with open-ended and vague answers. Unfortunately, the answers he provided to the villagers' concerns did nothing more than provoke more outlandish questions. Till now Tristin had done his best to keep out of this whole business; however, he also had questions pertaining to Darius' mission and decided to join in the attack.

Tristin climbed down from his tree and made his way over to the crowd, which had gathered around Heretius's home because Heretius had shut himself in. It appeared it would be impossible for him to get within a stone's throw of Heretius's house, for the villagers had surrounded any possible exit, or for Heretius any means of anyone entering his home.

Tristin had quickly given up hope of seeing Heretius, nevertheless trying to have a conversation with him. So slowly he made his way back to the large tree, which he and Darius had always played on, when he noticed a shadowy figure darting behind a row of bushes. Tristin was always very curious and instinctively he followed the figure trying to keep far enough back and well enough hidden as not to be discovered.

Silently the unknown figure moved from tree to tree and house to house as it made its way through the village. After a few close calls, and nearly causing himself to be discovered, they had both reached the edge of the clearing, and without hesitation the creature dove through the brush and out of Tristin's site. Hesitantly, and making sure to give the shadowy creature enough of a head start as to not discover him, Tristin slowly made his way through the heaviest parts of the bushes to conceal himself.

If Tristin had waited just a few seconds

longer he would have completely lost the trail of the shadow. Just as he breached the thick outer wall of the bushes, he noticed the tail of the shadow's cloak disappear into a perfectly concealed door in the side of a large Berkun Tree. An instant later there was no sign that anyone or anything had disturbed the tree or its surroundings.

Tristin waited some time, while sitting under the cover of the bush, wondering whether he should run and get some help or investigate the tree on his own. The tree was extremely old and the craftsmanship of the door was so precise that even close up it was hard to decipher any markings. So that would have to mean that most likely the secret door had to have been there for a very long time as well.

Tristin was trying to rummage everything through his head quickly enough as to not waste time, as he whispered to himself. "So, if this secret door has been here for a long time that would have to mean that this shadow guy has been here for some time as well. I mean it's not like he could have stumbled across anything like this. And he has never done anything to harm any of us, so he may not be bad. On the other hand, maybe he has been planning something all this time, and this tree is his lair. AHHH!!!!" Tristin accidentally let out a cry of frustration, and quickly threw himself to the ground under the bush waiting to see if anyone had discovered him.

Tristin hunched silent and motionless for about five minutes before making up his mind that no one had heard him. Then as quickly and silently as he could, Tristin dashed for the large Berkun and dove for the door. But, where was the door? Tristin looked franticly for any sign of a protrusion or some type of hinge, signifying its location, but nothing was found. "No, if only I had run for the door while it was still open, now what am I going to do?"

There was no sign of a doorknob or handle of any sort, so Tristin decided that the door must be opened by either magic or some hidden switch or lever, but where was it? Tristin quickly began to lose hope as he pulled on every branch and stub that was on or near the tree, and still the door remained closed. After searching for some time and creating quite a noise hitting the tree, Tristin turned and headed for home, "I'll come back later and give the tree another look over, maybe I can catch this guy when he leaves"! With his head hung low, Tristin was just about back to the clearing when he heard a squeaking noise behind him. Quickly he turned around to discover the door on the tree had been opened with the shadowy figure standing next to it, with his gaze fixed on him. Tristin's heart stopped cold in his chest, he was unable to move, petrified to the spot with fear. Yet, before he could force a reaction, the shadowy figure slowly raised his hand, motioning Tristin to follow him, and once again descended into the hollow of the tree. Tristin, although still filled with panic and fear, couldn't miss this opportunity to gain access to the tree, not a second time.

Tristin made his way over to the opening in the tree. His body was still tight with fear as he tried to will himself to enter the dark opening. Suddenly, the large wooden door began to close as if it had a will of its own. Without time to think, Tristin threw his body through the doorway just in time to hear the soft click of the door behind him. He swiftly collected himself and found that he was standing at the top of what seemed to be an extremely long and steep spiral staircase heading straight down into the earth. The shaft would have been completely black if it weren't for the sparse light that was given off by small candles that lined the stairwell.

The realization of what had just happened flooded Tristin's mind as he frantically searched for the door. It had just clicked shut behind him! Was it locked? Did it even matter if the door was locked if he couldn't find the handle! "Where did the door go!" There was only one path left for Tristin and he knew what he had to do. Slowly he began to climb down the stairwell. The stairs seemed like an endless descent which gave his eyes time to adjust to the darkness. Down and down Tristin climbed until he noticed a faint glow. The color of the light was different from that of the candles and it was coming out of a room at the bottom of the stairs.

The small room at the bottom of the long spiral staircase was relatively small and circular. Against one wall there was a fireplace that appeared to be built into the side of the enormous tree trunk. Within it, a fire was lit and a large black cauldron was bubbling over it. Across the room was a large bookshelf, which just like the fireplace had been built directly into the wall of the tree. The shelf which was packed with as many books as one could have possibly made room for. Also located next to the bookshelf was a large wooden trunk, which strangely enough had an enormous lock set upon it, yet the lock had no keyhole to open it. There were also two lamps on either side of the room whose light seemed to be reflected off the round walls making the room very bright in relation to the black stairwell. And finally, centered in the middle of the room was a large and very solid wooden table, which again like its wooden counterparts was carved directly from the tree. Sitting at the table was the shadowy creature, whom under the revealing lights, Tristin realized this was no mere shadow but someone under the cloak.

Tristin once again found himself glued to the floor, who could this hooded figure be? Even under the lights he couldn't make out any facial features, other than two bright glowing eyes that seemed as if they were reading Tristin's every thought.

Slowly the cloaked figure raised his hand, and at that moment the chair on the other side of the table slid back, as if guided by some magical force. Taking a deep breath, Tristin accepted the offer and sat down at the table with the cloaked being. Quite some time passed and not a word was said, but much information was passed between the two. Those two glowing eyes hidden beneath the dark hood prodded Tristin's mind with questions. Tristin could do nothing to defend himself from this mental attack, his eyes were fixed on those under the cloak, unblinking.

Finally, the onslaught ended, and for the first time the dark and mysterious being spoke. "Well, well, well, Tristin my lad, it seems that you've been through a lot these past two days, haven't you? But tell me this, if you were planning on pursuing your friend into the great forest, how would you help him? You've managed to quite literally take one step outside the safe haven of your community and tell your every last secret to the first creature you came across. Although your intentions may have been entirely noble, I don't know if you have what it takes to survive out there, much less be anything other than a hindrance to you friend."

Tristin's jaw dropped straight to the table, while his hand flew up slapping his forehead. "I can't believe I could be that stupid. Wait, how did you do that? Who are you, and what reason do you have to show any concern for either me or Darius?" Tristin jumped from his chair as the blood seemed to be flowing through him once again. He wasn't safe and every fiber in his being told him to run. As fast as his legs could move, he bolted towards the stairs, yet before he could reach the doorway hundreds of vines closed the gap. It appeared as if even the tree was against him and wasn't going to let him leave. Tristin suddenly burst out in terror, "It's a trap!"

Shaking his hooded head, the dark being continued. "I can't let you leave just yet, little one. Although we both know that there is nothing anyone can say to stop you from chasing after your friend. I'm hoping you might give me a few more moments of your life before you go and throw it away, it may be very beneficial to yourself, and quite possibly to Darius."

Realizing that staying might possibly be his only chance for getting out of this underground dungeon, Tristin hesitantly returns to his chair at the table.

"Ah very good", the hooded creature leaned back in his chair, seeming slightly more relaxed. "Now, first of all, I would like to ask you a question. Do you know why your friend Darius was chosen over all the other Grimps, or any of the other creatures in the forest for that matter?"

Suddenly, for the first time, Tristin let this very obvious question cloud his mind. He had never really thought of Darius as being lucky or special. Until yesterday when he learned of his friend's fate, Tristin had never been jealous of Darius' abilities. Through it all, that one thought had never crossed his mind, why? "Well I suppose," nothing, Tristin could think of no reason that Darius would be selected. He was of no importance when it came to family lines, and Tristin had never seen any special characteristics, or powers that would make him stand out. No, Darius was just an average grimp, nothing special. "Nothing special," Tristin had just realized that he had spoken out loud and quickly cast his gaze to meet that of the hooded creatures.

"Ha, precisely," replied the cloaked figure with a cold, almost lifeless laugh. "There is no real reason Darius was chosen over you or anyone else. You said it yourself, Darius was nothing special."

Tristin's eyebrows pinched together in anger at the ridiculing of his friend. "Your wrong, Heretius is the wisest Grimp in the world and if he said that Darius was the one there has to be a reason! So, don't talk about my friend in my presence ever again, I don't care if you can do little magic tricks, you don't scare me."

Suddenly, like a bolt of lightning, the realization hit Tristin. This cloaked figure was able to control magic! Tristin had never heard of anyone other than Heretius who was able to do that, at least no one still alive. But, even Heretius was too old to do much more than small tricks, he said it himself and that's why he sent Darius instead of going himself. "Who are you, and what are you doing here?"

"Don't you know? You've been thinking it ever since you started following me through the bushes up above. Oh come now, you don't think I didn't notice you behind me, you make more noise than giants walking through the forest in autumn. Then you were about to give up searching for the door to the tree until I came up to get you. Yet, still, you haven't made the idea stick of who truly lies beneath this cloak?"

The Berkun Tree

Tristin thought back recalling when he first caught sight of the shadowy figure darting behind the trees. He had been walking away from the crowd gathered around Heretius's house, heading towards his favorite climbing tree. "But, if you're who I think you are, then, then why? You must know the answer to the question better than anyone. Why Darius?

The two glowing eyes that had been transfixed on Tristin from within the hood of the cloak slowly faded away and with a nod of his head, the lights in the room became very dim. "The answer to your question is one of the most complicated questions of your time. Why should a young, innocent, and seemingly inconsequential Grimp such as Darius be chosen over the rest? Well, when you said Darius was nothing special, in a sense you were very right, and yet at the same time you could not have answered the question more wrongly. Because physically Darius poses no advantage over anyone else, actually if the decision were based on that, Darius would be one of the first out of the running. However, your friend has qualities that are neither inherited nor learned, at least not under the supervision of a village and family. No, Darius has a fire inside him, and that is something that hides deep within the mind; and that power, the power of thought is the most powerful of all. For although brute strength may win a battle, isn't it the strategy of the attack that determines the victor? When life has thrown you every possible hindrance and difficulty one could imagine, is it not the power of one's will that forces them to carry on? That, Tristin, is why Darius was chosen for this task. Nevertheless, no battle is ever won single-handedly. Think back to any story you have ever read or heard and you will see that the hero would never have made it through the first half of the story if it weren't for the interference of a friend and ally to help him seek his happily ever after. So, you see, you are much more a part of Darius's adventure than you may have thought. When he was chosen to this task, you were inevitably ensnared to the same fate. This is why I couldn't let you leave so quickly, for although Darius may be in dire need of your help even as we speak, you could do nothing to help him unless you are rightly prepared for the same journey, if not one filled with many more dangers. You Tristin, you are the bodyguard and protector of the chosen one. Now you must go and join your friend, but take with you these words. Your choices affect the outcome of the world, and your decisions at that moment of truth will not only change the lives of you and Darius, but will also influence every civilization on this planet. When you return from your journey the world will either be one whose path leads back to a serene and peaceful one, or it will be filled with the rage, malice and turmoil as the deepest depths release their hatred upon the surface. Also, take with you the knowledge of your own strength. Darius doesn't know, and you may not even realize this yourself, but yesterday while you two practiced your fire-making in the tent it was your combined efforts that created that fire, and not a single wizard. Now return to the surface, prepare for your journey, and tell no one of the tree, myself, or our discussion. Oh, and good luck my young friend."

After the cloaked figure had finished, both the lamps and the fire lost all their light and the room had grown dark. Tristin rubbed his eyes, which had grown sore after staring into that colorless hood for what seemed like an eternity. When he opened his eyes, Tristin found himself sitting at the base of the Berkun Tree near the edge of the forest. "Don't tell anyone? Like anyone would believe me!"

With that Tristin got up and hurried back to his house, which was empty since his parents had joined in the mass around Heretius's home. Quickly he gathered anything that he thought might be essential for a long yet fast passed journey, seeing as he had at least a half day's march in order to catch Darius.

After packing everything away, Tristin wrote a lengthy letter to his parents explaining that he had to leave and join Darius. With that Tristin headed out the door, and down the road past Heretius's house, where Tristin caught sight of Heretius trying to rid himself of the mob. The whole town was too occupied irritating Heretius with endless questions so there was no one to see Tristin off or bid him farewell. At length he reached the same stretch of path, which Darius' shadow had disappeared earlier that day, so he too began his journey into the forest. As Tristin looked back upon his village for the last time, he noticed a short, cloaked figure, waving goodbye to him. Returning the gesture, Tristin turned to follow that path of Darius, into the uncertainties and dangers of the forest.

Chapter 6

Trials of the Forest

The sun had just peeked over the horizon as its rays pierced through the branches of the trees. Darius had risen early in the morning to get a good start on the first full day of his quest. Unfortunately, little did Darius know that his early start not only caused him to have to tackle the journey on his own, but also meant he would cross the bridge at Tay's Crossing and reach Windover Lake long before Tristin could catch up, leaving him to the vital decision concerning which of the three paths he would choose.

However, Darius was unaware of Tristin's decision to follow him, so his early start was in the best of intentions. Darius figured that he should reach the bridge that spanned the Vahnulth River just as the sun was at its peak.

For poor Heretius, it was another day full of confusion and questioning; for not only was the purpose of Darius' mission still unanswered, but now the issue had arisen of another absent Grimp. Simultaneously, Tristin was now also engulfed in the same beautiful forest which beheld his best friend. And now the two of them, although unaware of each other's whereabouts, were both marching lightheartedly through the first stages of their adventures.

The time was passing easily for Darius. He had awoken as the first shards of sunlight peeked over the horizon and had been on the move ever since. It was now about midday and Darius' had just caught sight of the first major landmark on Heretius's map, just within his eyesight lay Tay's Crossing. Darius immediately knew that this would mean his journey was about to get quite a bit tougher, yet it was nice to see some similarity between his map and the actual path.

Darius had never actually seen the Vahnulth River so it was quite a shock to him when he first witnessed its massive size. The bridge that connected the two shores was also somewhat of a marvel to behold. It was not only very sturdy, but looked as if it once admitted large pulled carts and was capable of supporting armies of men at any given time. Luckily enough for Darius the bridge was also very wide, and since there was at least a hundred foot drop he was able to walk down the very center, keeping his eyes off the torrent waters below.

The remainder of the day's hike was fairly simple for both Darius and Tristin. It wasn't until nightfall that Darius received his first taste of what a journey through the forest really meant. The farther Darius ventured into the forest, the closer the trees grew together letting less and less light through their ensnaring branches. The sun had been out of Darius' sight for some time so he knew that it must be about time to call it a night. So, he quickly gathered as many loose twigs and as much dry grass as he could and set up camp. Using his now nearly perfected combustion spell, Darius was able to light his campfire. A full moon had risen high over the treetops casting an eerie shadow all around the poor grimp. The creatures of the night had come out from their hiding places and caused Darius to jump at every animal's call or the breaking of twigs far off in the forest. Before Darius drifted into an inevitable sleep, he could hear a familiar sound growing louder and closer to his camp. It was a sound Darius had heard only one other time in his life, he had heard it in a dream the night before he started his quest. It was the howl of wolves.

The ground was uncomfortable and the surrounding darkness was just about as much as poor Darius could bear. However, soon all things, terrible as they may seem, eventually come to an end. Darius had no trouble waking at the first hint of sunlight, since he was woken nearly every hour by the noises of the woods.

It was a gloomy morning as a light fog had rolled in, ensnaring the forest and blocking the few warm rays of the sun which penetrated the tree branches. Darius had to drag his body along the path, he had lost all his strength and his legs felt as if they were pushing him through a swamp. The forest was nothing like it had been the previous day. With the shrouding mists of a dense fog, Darius' vision had become quite limited. As the day grew on the fog simply got worse with each passing hour. An eerie calmness had beset the woods, and Darius had no idea how far he had traveled. There were no curves in the path, and the trees seemed to have no distinctions from one another. It appeared to Darius that he hadn't really gained any ground since he awoke; however, that was hours ago. Regardless, Darius kept walking trying to keep his mind focused on the path ahead.

Slowly a faded image of the sun, blocked out by an ever-increasing fog, passed across the sky. The forest seemed almost dead as a small grimp trudged further on, in hopes of reaching his next destination. There was no gentle breeze and the lively song that the woodland creatures once sang was dead with the forest. Not only did the fog create a lifeless calm, but it also acted as an evil veil drowning all the hopes and cares from the grimp. It was now well past lunch, but Darius had lost his will to do anything but walk. He was unaware that when he had awoken that morning, he had begun the first of many trials that would try and prevent the success of his journey, and he was losing. The fog that had overtaken the forest was actually alive, it was known as the Forest Mist, and was clouding Darius' mind with fears and failure. Darius was lost.

When Valley Elves were still very young, they were told the many stories of their heritage and reason for existence. Also, many of the tales they learned acted as warnings to keep them safe from their enemies. One of the very first tales any Valley Elf ever learns is that of the "Deadly Miasma". –

Once, long before the great wars, back before the

great forest was called Great, it was the dawn of the Age of Magic. There were two feuding families that lived among the forest, and since they were the first to successfully control the powers of magic it was a struggle for power. As the two families delved further into their supernatural abilities, the more destructive the feud became. The families had driven all other inhabitants out of the forest with their quarreling. However, one foolish little elf decided to investigate the families and is the only witness to the true end of the feud. It is said that the two families grew so great in their magic that it was undeniably their destruction. Both families thought they had found a magic spell to rid themselves of the other family, thus setting them up as the most powerful in the world. However, when the two families met along with their two magic spells, something happened. Instead of destroying one another as the families anticipated, the spells merged and formed a small translucent mist. Slowly the mist grew, engulfing the two staggered families and never were they heard from again. The tale also goes on the say that this "Deadly Miasma", a small veil of mist, follows the breeze and any unsuspecting fool who wanders into that mist is never seen again. The mist causes that unfortunate soul to lose all memories, hopes and dreams, and walk aimlessly to their death. Throughout the years, there have been only five known to have walked through the mist and return again to tell their tale, these five were the same that entrapped the Great Dragon, ending the Great War and the Age of Magic.

There were many dangers of the forest, and unfortunately Heretius never had ample time to prepare Darius for the bulk of them. Solemnly Darius marched on, he had lost all memory of his quest and the village he left behind. All that Darius had left was a deep sorrow and an urge to simply continue walking, neither of which he could explain nor did he care to try. The end had come far too quickly for the young grimp, as he was unaware of the closeness of his death.

Fortunately, Darius was either surprisingly lucky or had friends in the forest of which he was unaware. Just as he had completely given up and his spirit was about to fade into the mist, something unexpected happened. A sudden gust of wind took hold of the Forest Mist and cast it back into the heart of the forest. The fog was quickly lifted and with it the gloominess that had surrounded him. Darius felt as if he had just awoken from a very important dream, yet forgot what took place the moment he awoke.

"Where am I?" Darius found himself standing

amongst a small clearing off the side of the path. The grass was a lush green, and rows of beautiful oak trees acted as a fence around the clearing. There were many small berry bushes and fruit trees scattered about, and in the center was a gorgeous, sparkling blue pond. A large and old willow spread its branches over the pond providing a cooling shade for the small woodland creatures. Darius let his jaw fall open as he stood, gazing, collecting his thoughts. Nothing could have prepared him for the sheer beauty that lay before him.

"It's Windover Pond! I've found it!" Darius was overcome with joy. Quickly he walked over to the small pond and gazed into the crystal-clear water. Darius reached down into the water, cupping his hands and drew the water to his mouth. The water was as perfect as it looked, and for the first time Darius noticed how thirsty the journey had made him, he had been walking nonstop ever since he awoke and it was now evening.

Darius spent nearly an hour sipping the waters of the pond and eating the fruit of the bushes before he had his fill. Knowing that he couldn't possibly find a better place to camp, he decided to fill his pack with as much fruit and as many berries that he could fit and... "Where is it? I couldn't have... NO!" Falling to the grass with his head cradled in his hands, Darius realized that he never collected his things before he left camp earlier that morning. "How could I have been so careless, now what am I going to do? How stupid." Darius didn't have a choice he had to leave his pack behind. If he were to go back for it now, he would lose two days, and Darius didn't know how much time he had.

"Well, I guess I'll just have to make do without it." Darius gathered some soft ferns and made a bed in the grass. The journey through the fog drained all his energy, and if it weren't for the pond and the fruit trees Darius would have died even if the fog didn't get him. Yet, it was nearing evening and although the sun was still in the sky, he decided to call it a night.

Before Darius could lay his head on his fern pillow, he was startled by something rustling in the bushes. Thinking it was nothing more than a small creature caught in the branches of a bush Darius laid down and closed his eyes. Again, he heard rustling in the bushes on the edge of the clearing and again was about to dismiss it, when the noise was followed by a loud and deep cackle.

Darius quickly jumped to his feet and pulled his dagger from its sheath (the one item Darius still had after leaving his pack behind). Transfixing his eyes on the bush, Darius began to think of any and every horrible thing that could have made that laugh. There was still quite enough light so that he could see past the line of trees that made up the boundary of the clearing, and nothing was there.

Suddenly, an explosion of fire erupted from the ground. It was a constant blue flame and it was engulfed in a thick, black smoke. For a while nothing seemed to happen, although the fire was large and undying it neither consumed any of the bushes, trees, or grass, nor did it give off any heat. Darius caught sight of something moving in the center of the fire, but couldn't make out a figure due to the thickness of the smoke.

Darius became quite curious, he had never heard of a fire that didn't burn, so he thought maybe it was alive. "What are you?"

The fire, as if in response to Darius' question grew in size, and added to the blue were, red, yellow, and green flames. Although it was very beautiful, the thought of this sudden fire erupting from the ground made Darius very nervous and he slowly moved backwards towards the pond. While backing up, Darius again noticed something moving inside the flames, but what was it?

Darius backed himself up against the old willow tree. At least if this flame creature were to attack, he could dive into the water and save himself. Well, now what? The flame kept changing colors but did nothing else. Darius tried to think of some logical explanation for the flame. "Maybe there is some sort of underground lava spring. No, that can't be it, that doesn't explain it not being hot or burning anything." Well, maybe it just wasn't close enough to anything to burn it? Spotting a fallen branch near the edge of the clearing Darius decided to test this theory. However, before he could move for the branch, he caught sight of that same figure moving inside the fire. Only this time it began to move out of the flames and towards him.

It was a hooded creature of some sort, and as it stepped out of the flames it looked almost like a sorceress. Darius had never seen a wizard (that is, other than Heretius who was always dressed as a common grimp) yet he had heard descriptions of them by both Heretius and Tristin. All Darius could tell from this cloaked being was that it was most definitely the figure of a woman, and she must be capable of some sort of magic if she can stand in fire. The cloaked lady walked a few feet from her fire and as she did so the fire quickly died back into the ground. Darius tried to get up the nerve to ask this woman who and what she was, but was beaten to the questioning.

The woman's eyes were cold and dark, and were the perfect tools for inflicting fear. "Tell me little grimp, why is it that your trespassing on my land? Do you know what happens to those I find intruding on my property?"

Darius couldn't control himself from shaking. What was he going to do, he was no match for a sorceress, heck, he couldn't even beat a sorceress's apprentice! "I, I'm, err, I mean, I."

"Stop that infernal stuttering and tell me what you're doing here!" The cloaked woman's voice rang through the forest and pierced into Darius, making him even more nervous and scared them before.

Darius took a deep breath, closed his eyes, and began speaking as fast as his lips could create words. "My name is Darius, I was sent on a quest by Heretius a great and powerful wizard, and no one told me this land was owned by anyone, so please let me through or you will be the cause of the destruction of the world." Darius kept his eyes shut as tight as he could, waiting for the unjust hand of the sorceress to strike him down.

After a brief period of silence, the sorceress let out a long and wicked laugh, which sounded eerily similar to a woodland creature crying out in pain before its slaughtered. "So, you're the best that poor excuse for a wizard could dig up? I knew he was growing senile in his old age, but this is a little too much! Well my young grimp, I'm sorry, however I'm going to have to destroy you. That is unless Heretius has taught you any magic to defend yourself with."

"No, wait!" Darius was in trouble, the only magic he knew was creating a small campfire, but what effect would that have on a sorceress who could stand in fire? Darius was running out of time, all he could think to do was try and slowly back away, however he was already backed up against the old willow tree. The sorceress raised her arms into the air and started reciting some spell he couldn't comprehend. However, Darius wasn't about to wait around to see what the sorceress had in mind, so he quickly dove for the small pond. As Darius flew through the air he noticed a blinding flash behind him, and he realized the purpose of the flash immediately. Instead of gliding into the pond waters as one would expect, when Darius hit the pond he only sunk in up to his waist.

"Ahh, Quicksand!" Frantically Darius attempted to pull himself back to the shore, yet the harder he tried the faster he sunk in the sand. Darius began to scream for help which, although it may have been useless it was the first thing anyone would do in his situation. Nevertheless, it wasn't quite time for Darius to die as the most unlikely of friends came to his aid, even if it wasn't on purpose. Hanging directly over Darius's head was one of the branches of the old willow tree. Quickly, Darius caught hold of the branch and was able to pull himself back to land, postponing the wrath of the sorceress for a bit longer.

The sorceress watched as Darius lifted himself back to his feet. "Well Darius, it appears you have been blessed with a bit of luck! However, it's going to take more than petty luck to save yourself from my magic." Again, the sorceress raised her arms into the air and began reciting another spell.

After a few seconds, a shining ball of light appeared between the witch's hands. A moment later the sorceress cast the shinning orb at Darius, who this time could do nothing but close his eyes and wait for the inevitable.

The next few seconds seemed to last forever as Darius waited for his end. Nothing! Could she have missed? Darius opened one eye to find out what might have happened to the sorceress's magic. She was still standing there, with those cold evil eyes still drilling into Darius and half a grin, which had the same malicious characteristics.

Darius was now greatly confused, what happened to her magical spell? Maybe she was just bluffing and had shown off her only two real spells. Yet, once again Darius learned the foolishness of underestimating the forest. A small grin had found its way to Darius' face and he was just about to mock the powers of this so-called sorceress when he felt a stiff and rugged hand grab his shoulder. Without hesitation, Darius whipped his body around to discover the identity of his second assailant, and when their eyes met, Darius was once again aware of what true terror felt like.

The sorceress's magic was true to its mark, yet it wasn't Darius she was trying to hit. That ball of light did something that Darius had never thought possible, it gave life to the old willow tree and it looked mad. Darius was able to pull himself free from the willow's grip; however, as he did so, four more branch-like arms quickly surrounded him. Darius found that he still had his dagger in his hand; and, although it wouldn't seem a dagger would be very effective on a tree, he had no other weapons to choose from. So, Darius began swinging at the branches, trying his best to fend them off. Nonetheless, his dagger failed as it was knocked out of his hand and the willow seized Darius, lifted him into the air and began squeezing the life out of him. Gasping for air as the willow coiled tighter and tighter around him, Darius had the sudden realization that his attacker was merely wood.

"Fotia", quickly Darius set the branch of the tree ablaze, and although his small forest fire was only enough to singe its leaves it did the trick and Darius was released. Falling nearly ten feet Darius hit the ground and cut his arm open on the side of a rock. For the time, he had other things to worry about as he picked himself off the ground again, clutching his side after nearly being squeezed to death.

"Ha, ha, ha. Impressive." The sorceress was clapping and a large toothy grin was visible from within the hood of her cloak. Darius' near-death escapes seemed to be amusing her. Darius was enraged. He no longer cared about his quest, or his life for that matter, but he was determined to do anything possible to fight this witch. So, without considering the consequences, Darius quickly thought up the largest campfire he could imagine and focused it on the sorceress. "Let's find out if you can stand in real fire!" With a scream that echoed through the forest, Darius released some magic of his own, yet not the small campfire he was expecting. An enormous ball of pure translucent light was sent flying at the sorceress hitting her with an explosion that was felt back at the Grimp village, all while also throwing Darius backward off his feet and onto the ground.

Nearly a minute later, the smoke of the blast began lifting from the clearing, yet that familiar horrified look never fell from Darius' face. The sorceress, although obviously daunted, was still standing as her body was glowing with power and her eyes, now gleaming red, were piercing straight into Darius.

Then just as suddenly as the ball of power left Darius, the moment had ended, and the smile returned to the sorceress along with her vial laugh. "Well Darius, it seems Heretius may have been right about you after all, you seem to have a great power hidden inside yourself. I have decided to let you live so that you may continue your quest. However! We shall meet again Darius; you have my promise on that. And when we do meet again, rest assured we will finish this!" With that, the sorceress disappeared in the same manner by which she had arrived, a blast of fire.

The clearing was returned to its prior peaceful nature, and Darius, who was still exhausted after his struggle with the willow tree, collapsed onto the soft grasses near the pond and instantly drifted off to sleep.

Chapter 7

The Secret at Windover

It was a new morning, the third since Darius had entered the forest. The young Grimps body lay lifeless on the lush green floor of the woods. It was much later in the morning than Darius would have hoped for. When he left the sanctuary of this village his goal was to spend as many of the daylight hours as possible traveling towards his destination, in hopes of finishing his journey quickly and successfully. However, due to the trials the forest had beset him with the previous day he was merely lucky to still be breathing.

The prior day had been one blurred mess in Darius' mind. Slowly he opened his eyes, blinking them repeatedly, trying to clear the drowsiness of sleep from his mind. He clutched his arms tightly around his backpack in an attempt to make the ground a more relaxing spot to lie. Suddenly, like a roaring flood down a small creek, all the misfortunes of the prior day came crashing back into Darius' memory. A large old willow tree was hovering over Darius, as he scanned the clearing hoping he was alone.

"I've got all my stuff back! Was it all just a dream?" Darius remembered he had forgotten his things behind the previous morning, or had he? Quickly he pulled his body over to the pond, filled his hands with water, and threw it on his face. "Could I have dreamt the whole battle with the sorceress? I guess that would explain my pack still being with me, and that incredible blast I sent at that witch. But none of that makes any sense!"

Then, as Darius was washing his face in the pond waters, he noticed a large scar on his left arm. Like a jigsaw puzzle in his mind, all of the pieces slowly came back together. He recalled his battle with the willow tree and how he sliced open his arm after falling from its grasp. Darius then fell on his back, collecting his thoughts and the instances of the day before.

It was quite sometime before Darius rose to his feet to continue his quest. He found himself in much less of a hurry to continue through to his next potential trial. So quietly he sat himself back onto the grassy floor. As he ate his breakfast, which was now more of a lunch, he listened to the songs of the forest wildlife that once again filled the clearing.

After eating Darius decided to take the opportunity, since he didn't know if he were to have one again, to take a swim and bathe himself in the pond. Slowly he removed his shirt, gingerly pulling the sleeve over the wound on his arm, and placed it by his pack next to the willow tree.

As it was already late in the morning the sun had ample time to warm the air. Darius was about to simply dive into the pond waters when he remembered how it had turned to quicksand the previous day. So, he decided to slowly inch his body into the water, just in case. The water was beautiful, not only was it the perfect temperature, it was also crystal clear as Darius was able to see straight to the bottom which must have been twenty feet down.

Darius quickly forgot about the sorceress and the quicksand, the pond allowed him to relax and forget his troubles. Darius was just about ready to leave the pond and continue down the path when he noticed something moving in the waters. "Fish!" For the first time he realized that there were fish swimming in the pond with him. "Mmmm, smoked fish sounds really good!" Fish was somewhat of a rare delicacy in the grimp village, since the only source of fish came from the Vahnulth River and few in his village ever traveled that far from home. Darius had only heard the stories of the adults in the village spearing fish, but he grasped the general idea and decided to give it a try.

Darius swiftly fashioned a spear out of a large sturdy stick by tying his dagger to the end of it. Then, with his newly forged weapon in hand, Darius dove back into the pond. Twenty minutes later Darius had all but given up, it was much easier in the stories he'd heard, especially since he really didn't have any clue as to what he was doing. However, refusing to give up, Darius took one more deep breath and submerged back into the pond. As he searched the waters for his prey, he noticed three large crescent fish take refuge in what appeared to be a deep hole in the side of the pond wall. Darius immediately darted over towards the hole, thinking he had the fish trapped! However, as Darius neared the opening, he realized that this hole was actually the mouth of a cave.

Darius couldn't hold his breath much longer and had to make for the surface. As he pulled himself out of the water Darius noticed the sun at its peak in the sky. The realization hit him that it was now afternoon and he had lost nearly a half days hike.

Nevertheless, he couldn't give up on his fish, since now he knew where they were hiding out. Before reentering the water, he decided to remove his dagger from the spear, since he would have less space to maneuver inside the cave.

With one last attempt, Darius dove straight down towards the cave opening. Again, he noticed the crescent fish swim further back into the cave. "I have you now." As Darius swam merely a few feet into the cave the light of the sun was already blocked out. Amazingly though, the scales of the crescent fish provided a subtle glow allowing Darius to continue after them. The cave was very deep and Darius couldn't hold his breath much longer. He was about to turn back when the cave bent slightly, and he noticed an orangish light penetrating through the water up ahead. He had come too far now to make it back to the surface, so Darius decided to make for the light, hoping that he would find an air pocket.

Darius was running out of time and wasn't quite sure he could make it to the other end. As he neared the light at the end of the cave, Darius noticed a small band of crescent fish stuck at a dead-end in a very short inlet alongside the cave. It seemed as if they were mocking Darius. He could now have easily caught them, yet if he were to use his energy on the fish, he wouldn't make it to the caves end. It was now too late to catch the fish as surviving the swim took the lead on his priorities. With one last ounce of effort, he pushed himself as hard as he could to reach the strange light at the end of the cave. His vision began to darken as his oxygen supply was completely depleted. With one last surge, he kicked his body to the surfaced and let out a loud, deep gasp for air.

Now where was he? Slowly Darius' eyes began to focus in the darkness. It appeared that the underground cave continued on above the water. Eerie sounds of water droplets, falling from the cave ceiling and crashing to the floor, echoed throughout the cave. Darius pulled himself out of the water, and with dagger in hand slowly began to venture down the cave. It was unlike anything Darius had ever seen before. The strange light he had seen from the underwater cave appeared to be radiating off the stalactites above him.

This new cave was much larger than the one Darius had followed the fish into. The ceiling was three times his height and the walls nearly seven times his width. It was cold and damp in the cave, and the fact that Darius was wet and without his shirt didn't help matters. The cave was anything but straight, it seemed Darius couldn't take more than five steps before he was forced one direction or the other. Strange echoes could be heard from deep within the cave, and sounded almost like gruff voices. They were voices! As Darius rounded the next corner, he saw what looked like the light from a large campfire. Quickly Darius hid himself against the darkness of the wall and slowly continued on towards the light of the fire. The fire and the voices were coming from another cave off the side of the main tunnel. Darius slowly crawled along the next bend, making sure to stay hidden along the cave wall, and found himself right at the mouth of an enormous room. Directly in the center was a massive fire with an odd-shaped animal roasting over the top. On either side of the fire were two enormous creatures, which Darius immediately recognized as orcs. His heart fell straight to his feet, and his breaths were coming in short loud pants. Darius had heard many stories of the orcs, all consisted of the torturing and consuming of anything in their path. The orcs were easily five times his size, their skin was a swampy green, and their teeth looked like they could carve rock. They were generally gangly and clumsy. When they walked their long arms nearly touched the ground. They carried with them large war hammers and clubs, which they let drag behind them as they walked. But the orcs were said to live only in the...

"Oh no!" Darius then realized that the orcs might just be the least of his worries if he didn't retreat quickly. The tunnel had to be one of the hidden entrances to the lands below. Quickly, Darius started to crawl backward to get out of this cave as swiftly as possible. As he was backing out of the cave Darius noticed his dagger was reflecting the light from the campfire. Quickly, Darius hid his dagger back into its sheath, but it was too late. When Darius looked back up, he saw two large and evil eyes less than a foot in front of his face. The orcs had spotted him!

Darius knew his only chance for survival would be to make his way back to the pond. So, before the orc could react, Darius punched him square in the nose and ran as fast as his legs could carry him, back towards the entrance. A loud roar echoed through the tunnels, as the org cried out in rage. Darius could hear the footsteps of the beast behind him, and could feel his putrid breath steaming on the back of his neck. The orc was gaining ground too quickly; Darius wasn't going to make it! The now enraged orc was swinging his club wildly at Darius as they ran. Luckily, the grimp was just short enough that the blow from the orc's club just missed his head and instead rang against the side of the cave. The entire cave shook with the power and weight of the massive orc. Fear had propelled Darius to run faster than he ever had in this life. He could see the waters of the cave entrance just ahead! With one final leap Darius threw his body at the pond waters.

Time seemed to come to a stop, as Darius watched his body fly through the air with his pursuer only inches behind. Within that moment he had a sense of extreme clarity as if this moment were frozen in time. His body lingered motionless in the air, the only one of his five senses that seemed to be in his control was his sight. He scanned his surroundings as every aspect became unimaginably clear. Dozens of small caterpillar-like creatures hung from the stalactites in the cave. These creatures were the source of the orange glow that lightly illuminated the cave. Through the light Darius could clearly see the malice in his pursuer's face. Deep in the blood-red hated of the orcs eyes Darius could see the serene reflection of the pond he was trying eagerly to reach. As he continued to scan the room his eyes fell on the large wooden club traveling towards his body. Then all went dark.

High above the trees, soaring in the winds, a small blue-tipped hawk scoured the land in search of something it could call lunch. While scanning back and forth over the forest paths, it caught sight of something rather unusual for this part of the forest. Down below on the forest floor there was a creature nonchalantly walking west down the trail. For although this adult blue-tipped hawk could soar with the winds and fly just about anywhere, it had never crossed the great Vahnulth River and therefore had never seen the likes of a grimp.

It had been somewhat of a lonely, yet peaceful, last couple of days for Tristin. It was his third day in the forest, but everything seemed all too similar to him. With the exception of the bridge at Tay's Crossing, the forest never seemed to change. Tristin had no map of the forest so he had no idea what to expect ahead of him. He was also unaware of the fork in the path not much more than an hour's walk ahead of him. Still, Tristin knew he had to somehow catch up to his friend and from there on he would leave any vital decisions to Darius.

As Tristin marched further down the path the light of the sun quickly hid behind a cloud. The skies in the west were growing dark and the winds began to pick up. Tristin wanted to get as far as he could before stopping to take shelter from the upcoming storm so he quickened his pace.

As he hurried down the path Tristin came to a clearing alongside the road. Its features were somewhat dull due to the grayness of the sky. However, Tristin's eyes lit up with delight as he noticed numerous fruit trees and berry bushes as well as a pond to refill his water pouch. Trying not to waste what little time he had before the storm hit, he quickly rushed over to the trees and bushes and filled his pack and shirt, so he would have plenty to eat while it rained. As he was collecting fruit, Tristin noticed that a couple of the bushes were charred along with the surrounding grass, it looked as if there had recently been a fire or small explosion. However, Tristin didn't have time to contemplate over the bushes, so he quickly ran over to a large willow tree and dropped off his fruit. Then he quickly made for the forest edge and picked up a number of fallen branches and twigs, and also brought those back to the willow tree to set up as a shelter from the rain.

While Tristin was creating a shelter against the old willow, he noticed for the first time a pack hanging from one of its lower branches. After finishing his small lean-to, Tristin walked over to retrieve the pack as the first rains began to fall, so quickly he hurried back to his shelter to examine the pack. He was in no hurry since the rain looked as if it might last for quite some time, so he set the pack on the ground and began eating the fruit he had collected. After having his fill, Tristin then began to rummage through the backpack. There appeared to be nothing overly special about the pack, it contained the sort of items one would pack before embarking on a long journey, much like Tristin's pack. He found some rope, a small blanket, canned food, and as he neared the bottom of the contents Tristin pulled out a small rolled parchment. It was a map of the forest! Tristin could trace back over the path he had taken, and figured he must be at Windover Pond. However, the smile quickly fell from Tristin's face when he saw where the map led next.

"The road splits in three! No, how am I supposed to catch Darius now?" After studying the map for a while Tristin decided he would just have to make a guess as to which way Darius would have gone. "I am Darius' best friend after all, so who should know him better than me?"

The rains were showing no signs of slowing, so Tristin had no choice but to say goodbye to the third day of his journey and hope the fourth would be filled with a little more hope. The winds brought with them cold air, so Tristin was pleased that the pack he found contained an extra blanket. Quickly he gathered together some of the smaller twigs and branches he had collected and put them in a pile. Within a few moments, Tristin had made himself a small campfire that would assist in keeping him warm through the night. (After his three days in the forest and with the advice he had received back at the village from Darius and Heretius, Tristin had now perfected the art of fire-making).

Tristin then pulled out the blankets from

both his pack and from the one he found, unfolded them and covered himself up. As he was making himself comfortable, Tristin noticed something that instantly picked up his spirits. He recognized that the blanket he had taken from the pack belonged to Darius. "Darius!" Tristin instantly shot up from the ground hitting his head on the branches he had set up, and then ran out into the rain yelling Darius' name. "Darius, it's me Tristin! Darius! Darius! Where are you?" There was no answer, and Tristin began to imagine all the dreadful things that may have happened to his best friend.

Dripping wet, Tristin gave up calling for Darius and returned to his shelter. After fixing his make-shift tent and relighting the campfire, which had gone out due to him hitting his head on the ceiling. This created a hole large enough to allow the rain to land on his campfire and put it out. He then decided he would have to wait the storm out and hope that Darius would come back in the morning to retrieve his belongings. He quickly pushed from his mind the thoughts that anything bad were to have happened to Darius along with the terror that he might have to finish his quest for him, he would definitely not be looking forward to either.

Tristin spent the next couple of hours lying by his fire, trying to figure out what might have happened to his friend. It was now suppertime and the rains were still showing no signs of slowing. As the hours slipped away, sleep slowly overtook the young grimp. Unfortunately, even in his dreams he found no solace as he could constantly hear Darius calling for him, screaming for help, but Tristin could never find him. The night continued, along with the rains and the misfortunes for both Darius and Tristin.

Chapter 8

Tristin's Decision

       The rains had continued straight through the night, and although it had relinquished in the morning its gloominess remained. Nothing had been spared by the torrential rains, including Tristin and his fire, which had gone out shortly after he had fallen asleep. The constant dripping of water through the ceiling of his shelter had awoken Tristin. A pool of water had accumulated under him as he slept through the night leaving him utterly drenched. Not wanting to continue lying in a puddle of water Tristin decided to get up and survey the land, hoping to find some sign of Darius.

       The trees in the clearing looked as if they were recovering from a great battle. Their mighty branches, which had once been raised high showing off the trees marvelous fruits, were now sagging humbly as if in defeat. The great rains had also taken their toll on Tristin who couldn't seem to shake off the coldness that was accompanied by the rain. Even the once crystal-clear waters of Windover pond had been clouded due to the tempest.

The day was not starting out well for Tristin, yet he knew he couldn't let the forest get to him. So, he decided to sit down, eat some breakfast, and determine what should be done about Darius and his unfinished quest. Quickly, Tristin gathered some of the fruit that had fallen due to the storm and sat down with Darius' map. Tristin knew what had to be done, however, he was reluctant to give up on his friend so quickly. There was no telling what sort of dangers Darius could have gotten himself into and Tristin couldn't leave him behind. The only problem was that Tristin had absolutely no idea as to where Darius could have gone. Why would he leave behind his stuff, unless he was in danger or in a great hurry?

Tristin's choices grew even more difficult as he studied the map of the forest. "Three paths! Which way would Darius have taken?" Tristin was having trouble concentrating on the map, there were too many other questions and concerns flying around his head. "No matter which path I choose I'm letting people down!" Tristin knew his choices but both made him sick. Should he risk temporarily abandoning the mission? This could let the entire world down if he and Darius were to fail. But he couldn't simply let his best friend be consumed by the dangers of the forest. "This isn't fair." Before he knew it Tristin had eaten all the fruit he had gathered, so his breakfast and time of procrastination had run out, it was time to choose. "Ok, I'll do it!"

Things weren't looking any better in the grimp village. Heretius was still unable to leave his home, or even open a window for that matter. He was under constant supervision as the adults of the village took shifts patrolling his house, waiting for answers. They had even, on the second day, attempted to break into Heretius's home but found the doors and windows impossible to breach.

The village had been at a standstill ever since Darius' departure, and when the village caught word of Tristin's disappearance the adults went into a panic. All the children of the village were suddenly under the strictest of supervision, and were normally kept in groups which suited them just fine.

It was the fourth day since Darius and Tristin had left the village and each of the first three days Heretius attempted to talk to the grimps, and every day was met with failure. Heretius was hardly able to speak a word before he would be ambushed with more questions and irrational concerns. The grimps of the village were still unaware of the true meaning behind Darius' leaving and wouldn't except Heretius's frail excuses or half-answers.

There was currently a total of five grimps in the village who knew the truth. Tristin's parents were now included in that group and could always be found with the parents of Darius trying to comfort one another.

The gloominess that hovered over Windover pond seemed to have found its way to the grimp village. Heretius knew that something had to be done to raise the spirits of the grimps, but what? The truth would send them into a panic and he could think up no other acceptable explanations. Still, something had to be done quickly before the villagers decided to take matters into their own hands.

After three days of agonizing over the details, Heretius decided he would have to tell the villagers the true reason for the absence of Darius and Tristin. His plan was to leave out as many of the more important details that he could in hopes of preventing a mass hysteria amongst the villagers. With that decided, Heretius walked over to his kitchen window and summoned a few grimps who were on guard duty. "Hello friends, would you be so kind as to gather all the grimps and bring them to my home within the hour. For then I will reveal the truth behind my most recent deeds."

Immediately, the eyes of those listening lit up and they quickly scattered in every direction to spread the word. Heretius chuckled to himself as this small act finally left him unguarded as those responsible to watch him all ran off at the news. Still, Heretius knew this had to be done and awaited his audience. It took no less then fifteen minutes for the entire village to gather outside Heretius's door. He was hoping to have a little more time to prepare his speech, but he would have to make do. Heretius had access to the roof of his house through a door in the attic. So, taking advantage of this, he decided to address the people from there.

There was much chatter among the grimps, they were all very anxious to finally learn the true meaning of the young grimps journey. Had it been anyone else who had sent the two away it might merely have been overlooked and considered unimportant. However, since it was at the village elders command that Darius (and, as far as the grimps knew, Tristin) were to leave the village it had to be something greatly important that would also concern all the grimps. This is why the villagers were being so persistent in knowing the truth.

A sudden hush fell over the crowd when they noticed Heretius hovering over them from his rooftop. Waiting a few moments to ensure he had the full attention of all the grimps, Heretius began.

"My friends, the answer which you have all gathered around to hear isn't nearly as simple as you or I would hope it to be, so please bear with me without interruptions." The crowd was deadly silent, some were even holding their breaths to avoid the noise an exhale would have made. "First of all, I would like to make it clear to each of you that never once did I tell either Darius or Tristin that they HAD to leave. What I presented before young Darius was a choice, an option that he could just as simply refused. I want you all to hold that in your memories because his decision was in your interest. As for Tristin, he was never offered that choice given to Darius, his path was chosen out of pure and true friendship. Now I want you to remember also, that what I placed before Darius is very complex, so listen fully before you react. As you all know, times have greatly changed since I was a young grimp! However, since then, not all creatures have taken this same path. You are all familiar with the story consisting of the Great Dragons and those stories pertaining to the end of the last great age, The Age of Magic. The task that I have sent Darius off to accomplish is twofold. Firstly, he is to rediscover our past, and in doing so put an end to the evil magic that was locked away these many years' past. Second, a task that neither Darius nor Tristin are aware of is much simpler, and also much, much more complex. They are to discover a name for our great age, and only by embarking on a great quest can they achieve this. As I said, there is no simplicity behind this quest, so I cannot simply state to you their objective, for not even I am fully aware of them all. What I must now ask of each of you is this. Leave the journey to those who it has been chosen! But that does not mean they must be alone on their quest. We must do our best in reestablishing that which our ancestors lost during the great war, friendship among those whom dwell in this forest with us. Now I to must leave you, and before you try, know that there is nothing you can say or do that will prevent me from doing so. Now leave, and do your best in creating a better future for the grimps to come." With that Heretius disappeared back into the sanctuary of his home.

The villagers all stood around speechless for some time, as if in shock by the news. Did Heretius say he was really going to leave them? Truth was, none of the grimps had ever made any real decisions without first consulting their village elder. How were they going to follow out Heretius's wishes without his leadership? After a seemingly endless silence, the villagers slowly made their way back to their homes.

A dim light coming in from a small window lit the way for a cloaked figure. He was rummaging through a large trunk and was quickly packing away oddly shaped items into an old shoulder bag. He then walked over to a dusty old cupboard, hidden in the wallboards, and pulled out a rather old and crooked walking stick. With that, the cloaked figure slipped out the back door of his home and disappeared into the forest. None of the grimps saw Heretius escape from the village, and it would be a long time before they where they were to witness anyone of his likeness again.

It was late in the morning and the gloomy remains of the storm still lingered in the air. Tristin could still make out the clearing of Windover Pond, now far behind him. He had decided to continue Darius' quest for him, or at least make it to Theshius where he could enlist her aid.

Not far ahead, Tristin could see where the path split, and a very dangerous choice had to be made. Should Tristin attempt the shortest path through the cave of Arem, or lose a couple of days by attempting the more simplistic and overly safer route. Then again there was the path to the north, but the thought of climbing the cliffs of Shemod, and having to cross the River Onyx wasn't all that appealing to Tristin. It didn't take long before he had reached the crossroads and the choice had to be made. In the end, it was the path of stealth that prevailed. Tristin was hoping that if he could quickly get through Arem's Cave the worst might be behind him. So, after quite a bit of hesitation, Tristin continued west toward the path towards Arem.

Chapter 9

An End, Followed by a Beginning

There was a musty scent in the air that was mixed with the lingering and foul odor of the orcs. Slowly, Darius' memories were coming back to him. He wasn't quite sure where he was; however, he wouldn't likely be forgetting how he got there. Horrifying images flashed through his head as he recalled running through the tunnels trying to escape the clutches of the brutish orcs.   He then remembered making one final lunge for the waters of the pond when the orc's club struck its mark, throwing Darius into the wall, knocking him unconscious.

Darius now found himself trapped inside a

small wooden cage hanging from the ceiling in a large stone room. Numerous animal carcasses were scattered about on the floor with the most recent still smoldering over a large fire. The room was fairly empty with the exception of a large pile of animal bones. The large fire, which rested in the center of the stone room, seemed to be the only source of light, and Darius couldn't quite figure out what was keeping it burning. There was also no sign of the orcs that had caged him, although their pungent odor suggested they weren't too far off.

Even with the assistance of the fire, the room was still very cold. It didn't help matters that Darius was without his shirt, which he had taken off before swimming in Windover Pond. However, the temperature was the least of Darius' worries since he knew if he didn't act quickly, he would be next on the orc's menu. The thought of burning his way through the wooden cage instantly came to his mind. This was followed by the immediate realization that the drop was well over five times his height, and he wouldn't be able to escape if he were wounded. Darius frantically searched the room, looking for anything to help him escape. It was then that he noticed his dagger lying on a stone table at the other end of the room.

"If only I could reach my knife, at least then I could cut through this cage and make the drop less painful."

Time was quickly running out for Darius. He could hear the voices of the orcs growing closer and he knew there was no way he would be able to take on a full-sized orc, not with a simple flame spell as the only weapon in his arsenal. He had no other choice, quickly Darius started to burn open the door of the cage, trying to keep the fire under control so the whole cage wouldn't ignite. Unfortunately, the wood of the cage was old and dried out. As the first spark made contact with the wood the cage was immediately engulfed in flames. The fire quickly crawled up the side of the cage and began to burn through the rope that had been suspending it. There was nothing Darius could do now but watch and wait as he was engulfed in his own fire.

Snap! The weight of the cage on the burning rope caused it to break sending it crashing to the floor. A large roar echoed through the cave as the cage struck the ground, shattering into numerous pieces. Darius was mostly uninjured, with the exception of many minor scrapes and bruises, and immediately he ran for his knife.

When the orcs had heard the sound of the cage hitting the ground they immediately came running, and were just in time to see their latest catch stealing back his dagger and running out a tunnel on the opposite side of the room. "Arrgh! Dinner getting away, quick catch it!"

Darius knew there was no way he could outrun the orcs; they were too large and knew the underground corridors too well. Darius once again found himself trying to escape, only this time he didn't know where he was running. The light from the fire quickly died out behind Darius, and was replaced by the fowl screams of his pursuers. The underground tunnels seemed to randomly project off in every direction. Darius tried using this to his advantage, turning whenever possible, to prevent the orcs from having a straight path to follow.

There was something unusual and very special about the rock from which these underground caverns were cut. Although the tunnels were very damp and cold, the rocks always felt warm. It also seemed as if these rocks were able to create their own light, providing a light blue glow, which illuminated the tunnels.

Now Darius was relying primarily on the darkness of the tunnels to help conceal him during his escape, he had no way of knowing the rocks would steal the darkness from him. No matter how many twists and turns Darius took, he could hear the heavy stomping of the orc's feet always one turn behind him. Darius knew he couldn't run much further, his short legs had to move three times as fast as the orcs and it was quickly draining his energy.

The orcs were cursing at Darius, and throwing small rocks whenever the cave allowed them a straight shot. It was then that Darius made his most fatal mistake. While looking back at the orcs and trying to dodge the rocks, Darius missed his turn. Smack! Darius turned his head forward just in time to see the wall slam right into his face. Once again everything went black, and Darius was knocked unconscious, unable to defend himself from the savage orcs.

A cold, gray mist filled the skies, along with Tristin's heart. He felt as if someone had stuck him with a dagger and the sensation kept digging further and further into him. Tristin had no idea as to what had become of his best friend. However, he couldn't shake the feeling that if he had only left the village sooner, he may have caught up to him in time to help him, wherever he was. Nevertheless, Tristin had made up his mind that he would have to finish Darius' mission, regardless of the fate he would undoubtedly face.

The path that led to the Caves of Arem could hardly be called a path. The road was overrun with grass and weeds, and if it weren't for the patches of ground that remained barren after centuries of travel Tristin would have been lost. Although the grass and weeds were thick and lush, the trees looked as if they had all died many years ago. The long-outstretched branches bore no leaves, and their bark was black and brittle. There was no wildlife to be seen or heard in this section of the forest, even the birds high up in the clouds kept clear of these dead woods. A sudden chill ran up Tristin's back, he had an unnerving feeling that he wasn't alone. He felt as if the trees were following his every movement and were just waiting for the right moment to grab him. What was left of the path was quickly becoming much narrower as the trees grew larger and closer together.

A light wind cut through the baron trees with ease and Tristin could faintly hear the cries of battle and the clashing of swords. It was coming from all around him, screams of the wounded followed by shrieks of some foul creatures as they destroyed their prey. Gradually the sounds grew louder and the battle drums echoed inside his head. Tristin threw his hands over his ears and dropped to his knees, "Go away, Leave me alone!" Louder, and louder the noise grew, as the tree branches seemed to move closer and closer to Tristin reaching out towards him. He could hear the screams of retreat, the minions of darkness were closing in from every side! The dead trees had trapped Tristin. He could hear the screams of all the evil creatures upon him! He then felt the weight of a hand clench his shoulder. This was it; Tristin knew he was finished but couldn't go down without a fight.

"Nooooooo!" Taking hold of a stick lying on the ground near him, Tristin spun around knocking his attacker off him. A small body flew from Tristin's side and landed next to one of the black trees.

The sounds were gone. The trees, although still black and dead, had withdrawn back from the path leaving a rather large and free road. Yet, the horror found its way right back to Tristin as he noticed two eyes hidden within the grass, gazing right into his own. "Ahhh! Stay back!" Tristin instinctively threw himself backwards away from the creature.

From behind the grassy shield came a soft and soothing voice. "Careful my friend, careful carful carfully, you must carry with you a great burden if you let the forest consume you so easily. Mmmhmmm."

Slowly the creature revealed himself from behind the heavy grass. Tristin didn't quite know what to make of him, he had never seen or heard of a creature such as the one standing before him. Two

112

large oversized eyes protruded from its deep purple skin. Although the creature stood upright, which made him about a head shorter than Tristin, he looked as if he would be more comfortable moving around on all fours. It also appeared that his body was completely covered, from his neck down, by a short thick purplish-blue fur. And to complete the comical appearance of the creature he wore a dark green jacket which not only hung down to his knees, but the sleeves were longer than his arms. Curiously the creature circled Tristin while humming a strange tune to himself. When he finally broke the silence and spoke to Tristin the creature had an equally inquisitive speech, it was almost as if his mouth couldn't quite keep up to his mind as he constantly repeated words as he spoke.

"Hello, hello, hello! My name is Keeris. Hmmm, who are you? What are you? Strange yes, hmm, yes quite peculiar!

Tristin wasn't exactly sure what this creature was or what to make of it, however it didn't appear hostile. "Umm, my name is Tristin, what exactly are you, and why are you hanging around this awful place?"

"Nice to meet you Mr. Tristin, I am a Kolerunt and this awful place is my home. It's very strange, very strange to see anyone using these paths nowadays, especially two in the same day, yes very odd indeed."

Tristin immediately sprung to life after hearing that someone else was recently spotted on this path. Could it have been Darius? "Tell me Keeris, whoever it was that you saw earlier on this path, what did he look like?"

Keeris began jumping around with an oversized smile on his face; it seemed this Kolerunt perceived everything as a game. "He, or it could have been a she, yes he or she hard to tell which, was about your height and stature, and kept well covered under a dark cloak. I wanted to say hi, I did I did, I don't often have visitors, but it seemed in a great hurry and I felt it carried with it an unfriendly burden, mmhmm." Keeris stopped jumping around, and began studying Tristin's face and his reaction to the news.

It appeared as if Keeris's cheerfulness was contagious, as Tristin suddenly couldn't stop smiling. "Keeris! This creature you saw, it must have been my best friend, and I thought I had lost him forever. Tell me, how long ago was it that he passed by here?"

Again, Keeris began jumping around Tristin. "Good, goodie, good! I will go with you, yes! It will be a quest for your no longer missing friend, what fun we will have, fun will have!"

"But..." Before Tristin could object to the company, Keeris disappeared back into the tall grass from which Tristin had first seen him. Slightly confused, yet happy to hear about the wellbeing of his friend, Tristin resumed his journey in hopes of catching up to Darius.

Tristin wasn't able to get very far before he was ambushed from overhead.

"Look out Mr. Tristin." It was Keeris, and he had jumped from a branch hovering above Tristin and landed not more than a foot in front of him. Keeris was still bearing a huge smile along with a walking stick and a pack, which was thrown over his shoulder. "You're quite a bit faster than I would have expected, I shall do better at keeping up, yes I will!"

"I don't think it's a good idea that you follow me, my real quest isn't to find my friend and it will undoubtedly get very dangerous."

Keeris pretended not to hear Tristin and started walking down the path. "Quick, quick, quick, yes you better walk faster than that if you ever want to catch up to your friend." As Keeris walked he added a dancing skip to his step, he seemed a little overly excited given the circumstances.

An End, Followed by a Beginning

Tristin immediately quickened his pace to catch up to Keeris. "I'm sorry for calling your home an awful place, but, well, why is it that you live out here by yourself?"

"Well Mr. Tristin, this here this is where I was born, therefore it's my home, and I never said I lived by myself. Speaking of being by yourself, by yourself, why is it that you're out in these woods all alone, mmmhhhmmm?"

"Well it's sort of a long story; however it may be a while before we catch my friend so I suppose I have the time to tell it, it will be nice having someone to talk to anyway." Tristin and Keeris spent the rest of the day walking down the forest path, exchanging stories about how and why they were in the forest. Quite some time had passed and neither one of the two traveling companions had realized just how late it had gotten. The sun had all but fallen over the horizon, and it would soon be getting very dark. The time had caught Tristin by surprise and he immediately began to scrabble in search of wood to start a fire.

"Friend, what are you doing? You don't happen to, happen to change into some strange and irregular creature once the sun goes down, do you?" Keeris began to laugh at his own joke and barely heard Tristin's response.

"You should know these woods, and more importantly the creatures in it, better than anyone. It's nearly dark and I need to quickly gather wood to make a fire before we lose the sunlight."

"Oh, is that all? Well, well, well then forget gathering wood and come with me, we're safer above, mmhhhmm."

Reluctantly, Tristin dropped the kindling he had gathered and followed his new friend over to an old large tree that had made its home alongside the path. In the blink of an eye Keeris scrambled up the tree and disappeared within a thicket of branches. Luckily for Tristin he was well experienced in the art of tree climbing. Although he may not have been as graceful as the Kolerunt, he managed his way up into the branches all the same.

It took quite a while before Tristin was able to find a branch he thought would not only be as comfortable as possible, but also large enough to hold him securely. Eventually, Tristin found a spot he liked and settled in for the night.

"Umm, Mr. Tristin, I believe I understand, understand the whole ordeal about your quest and all, but where exactly, where exactly were you headed before we ran into each other, mmhhmmm?"

"Alright. First off, enough with the whole, Mr.

Tristin, okay? After I thought I would never see Darius again, I decided to finish his journey for him. In his bag that I found abandoned at Windover Pond was a map with three paths which all led towards the Swamps of Kilvay, which is where I need to go. It was then that I decided that it would be best if I get to the swamps as quickly as possible, I'm pretty sure it's what Darius would have done. So, I headed down the path which led to the Caves of Arem and that's where I met you."

"Hodily-Ho! You really must have let the forest get into your head, yes into your head, and for quite some time! Especially if you started out heading for the mountains, mmhhmmm!"

"Why do you say that?"

"Well," Keeris's head dropped down from above Tristin with the same familiar smile smothered across his face. "If it's the caves that you headed for, headed for your not making very good time! I would guess, yes I would guess you are just as far from the caves now as you were when you left Windover Pond, ha, ha, ha!"

Tristin immediately reached for his map and began to look it over. "How could I have missed the caves there is only the one path leading towards them, how could I have possibly strayed off course?"

Tristin's hand unconsciously flew to his face smacking himself square in the head.

"Well Mr., err, well Tristin, there is much much much you need to learn about the forest if you hope to catch your friend, finish your quest, and get out to tell the tale, mmhhmmm. First of all, the forest paths don't often remain the same from one day to the next, no they don't! Secondly, you might as well simply have given up, given up, given up and gone home if you planned on making it through Deaths Doorway alive! Names are given out with reason behind them, you probably shouldn't forget that, shouldn't forget that! Deaths Doorway isn't a place to be traveled if you don't fully have your wits about you, nope, nope, no it's not, many more have lost themselves in these woods than the number who have successfully passed through that place alive, mmhhmmm."

"Well that's just great, so this map is pretty much garbage?"

"No, no, I don't think you should blame the map, nope not the map. The paths may not lead where they once did, but the landmarks are the same as they always were, and in the same place, yup, yup, yes, they are. Oh, and if you had known about the paths, you may have tried to cut straight through to the caves, straight on through. Bad danger there, not only would you have killed yourself in the process, but you would have neither met me, nor found your friend! Well at least found out he is still alive anyway, mmhhmmm. A little advice before sleep. Greatest grandad taught me, everything that happens brings with it both bad and good, you'll be better off if you always search out the good but learn from the bad."

Tristin's mind began surging with more and more questions; however, the forest had taken its toll and sleep had overpowered him. He decided if any of the questions were important enough, he could ask them in the morning. Hopefully, with his new guide, Tristin could quickly catch up to Darius and get through the swamps before long. An eerie darkness, which Tristin had felt shortly after leaving Windover Pond, seemed to slowly gain ground on him, which more so added to his urgency to seek out Theshius and Darius. Yet, all thoughts of the goods and evils of his quest were soon replaced with the peaceful darkness of sleep.

Chapter 10

Pleeris Valley

It was the fifth time the sun had risen over the horizon since both Darius and Tristin had left the security of the grimp village. A thin ray of sunlight had managed to find its way through the thick and enfolding branches that hid Tristin from the world. Slowly, Tristin's body came back to life. It was the first morning since he crossed the Vahnulth that he was able to recall instantly where he was and how he got there. Cautiously, making sure not to fall off his tree branch bed, Tristin let out a long, loud yawn while stretching the muscles in his arms and legs.

"Morning Keeris, sleep well? Keeris? Hey Keeris where are you?" Tristin quickly climbed up to the branch where Keeris had been sleeping, but he wasn't there. After searching over the tree Tristin

climbed down and started to survey the land.
"KEERIS! HEY KEERIS WHERE ARE YOU?"

"Well no wonder, no wonder, you have to build
a fire to protect yourself at night. With the noise
you make in the morning every creature within ten
miles ought to know you're awake, mmhhmmm!"
Tristin was relieved when he saw a familiar set of
oversized eyes and a huge smile pop its head out from
behind one of the larger trees. "Oh, come get some
food, Mmm, eat, yes food good, Mmm."

Content that nothing had changed overnight,
Tristin slowly made his way over to Keeris taking in
the beauty of the morning forest. The morning was
the best Tristin had spent since entering the forest
and the food, as well. The two new friends decided
to take it easy before they would embark on the first
day of their journey together.

"So, Mr. Tristin, I was thinking that, even
though you had your heart set on traveling through
the Caves of Arem, not a smarty move, maybe it
would be wiser if you follow the map over the White
River to the swamps, mmhhmmm?"

"That sounds like a good plan. However, I've
been told that it's not wise to stray from the forest
path, we could get lost forever! Oh, and would you
please stop with the whole mister thing already."

Keeris tilted his head slightly and his smile seemed to get even larger at the mister remark. "That's true, yup true true, but I will say our survival chances are much higher if we stay in the trees as opposed to the cave. Besides, I've lived in the forest my whole life and I've never gotten lost traveling off the path. Also, according to your map, if we make a straight path to the southwest, we can't really miss the White River, can we, nope?"

"I hope you're right Keeris. The way you put it pretty much anything is better than walking through Death's Doorway anyway."

"Good, good it's settled then. Let's go."

Tristin was quite reluctant, but once he let the path out of his sight a small burden was lifted off his shoulders. Walking amongst the trees with his new friend, Tristin was the happiest he had been since before he learned of Darius' quest, but his thoughts kept turning back towards Darius, wondering if he was alright, or even if he were still alive.

Having Keeris as company made the day not only go by faster, but also made it much more enjoyable. The morning went by rather quickly as the two walked through the forest, asking and answering each other's questions. It was soon time for lunch so they found a comfortable spot and stopped to eat.

"So Keeris, how long do you think it will take us to reach the White River?"

"Well, hmm yup yup judging by your map I would say about the time we're ready to stop for supper. From there, if we make good time and keep our meals short, I would think we could reach this Theshius's house in another full two days, maybe two in a half, mmhhmmm."

Far off in the distance, far under the depths of the planet's surface, a low pounding noise could be heard. The noise, the low beating hum of great battle drums slowly increased in numbers and magnitude. The world of Broudiun had suddenly come alive, as if some great power had awakened the whole of the Dark Realm from a great sleep and cast it into the heat of a great war. The forces of evil were being gathered together, it was a likeness that had not been matched since the Great War, which had ended the Age of Magic. Again, it was beginning.

The forest had undergone quite a distinct change from the way it had appeared to Tristin when he followed the path. Cutting directly through the forest was also much harder traveling, they didn't have the simplicities of the flattened path to guide them, instead they had to endure the uneven terrain and the constant attacks by branches and thorn bushes.

A few hours had passed since the two had stopped for lunch. The forest terrain was taking its toll on Tristin, which not only caused him to tire quicker but also caused the two to travel much slower than Keeris had anticipated, potentially adding another day before they were to reach Theshius.

A sigh of relief came to Tristin as he caught his first glimpse of what looked like a clearing ahead which would promise to make for some easier traveling. Tristin, who had begun to lose interest in the hike was walking with his head down and nearly ran right over Keeris, who had stopped and perked his ears.

"Mr. Tristin, shhh." Keeris squinted his eyes and slowly began scanning the surrounding forest, then lowered his voice to a barely audible whisper. "Tristin, did you hear anything just a bit ago? Something that sounded like a twig snap and leaves ruffle?"

"Keeris what has gotten into you? There have been rabbits and squirrels running past us constantly since we left the path."

"No, I think..." Keeris stopped and slowly backed up till he was in line with Tristin. "Buddy, if you've picked up any decent magic tricks, magic tricks now would be a good time to try and impress me, mmhhmmm."

"Keeris you're starting to scare me, what are you talking about?" It was just then that Tristin first noticed the shadow of some creature dart behind a larger tree off to their left. "What is that?"

"It's a colivien, there are three of them, two to the left and one to the right."

Taking a step back and lowing his voice till it matched Keeris', Tristin replied. "Are they dangerous?"

"I don't really know, I've never met up with one when they had the upper hand, usually they are nomads and keep to themselves."

Slowly Tristin and Keeris backed away from the colivien as Tristin began to reach for his dagger. Just as Tristin had pulled his dagger from its sheath a low and rough voice came from behind them. A fourth colivien had managed to slip in behind the two travelers and caught them by surprise. "Little grimp,

I would advise you to put the weapon away before I give the signal to those in the trees to release their arrows."

Hesitantly, Tristin returned the dagger to its home, clenched his eyes, and turned to meet the owner of the gruff voice. It was then that Tristin saw, for the first time, what a colivien looked like. This colivien appeared to be the leader of the small clan. If one were to categorize this creature, he would be most like an elf in both size and in his ability to use the forest as a cloak. However, the beauty and fairness which the elf was gifted bore no resemblance whatsoever to the colivien. He was nearly a foot taller than Tristin and about three times as wide. In no aspect did he appear weighted by his bulk; he was padded well with muscle, which gave him an advantage when it came to intimidating Tristin and Keeris. To top it off, his face was covered with a thick beard and his body with the skins of numerous animal hides.

Taking a few steps closer to the now frightened intruders, the leader of the colivien group continued. "Answer me this, why would a grimp cross the Vahnulth River and travel all the way to the Pleeris Valley, and accompanied by a Kolerunt nonetheless? Well, speak up!"

Tristin turned his gaze to Keeris looking for

some help, but none was given. Not wanting to anger
the colivien anymore than was necessary Tristin
spoke.

"Well, you see, ummm, it's kind of a long
story..."

"Why don't you just sum it up for me, okay."
The colivien was growing overly impatient with
Tristin.

"Okay, well I'm not really supposed to be
here, but I came after my friend who was sent on a
quest by Heretius, only I lost........."

"Wait!" The colivien moved in even closer to
Tristin, staring unblinkingly straight into his eyes.
"So, the old wizard is still alive after all these years,
and well, I would presume?"

Tristin kept his nervous filled eyes connected
to the colivien for some time before he realized he
had just been asked a question. "Oh, umm, yes,
Heretius is well."

The colivien leader let out a loud and hearty
laugh and then signaled to the archers in the trees.
Both Tristin and Keeris thought that meant the end
for them both, however they realized shortly after
that the others had just been summoned over to the
leader.

"Right then, my young intruders, your trivial lives will be spared for now. However, you are now my prisoners and will accompany me back to my village, there we will determine your fate.

The next hour was very solemn and quiet, as neither Tristin nor Keeris dared speak. The six colivien made a circle around their prisoners as they escorted them back to their village. Tristin was amazed at the colivien's sense of direction; it would have appeared to him that they were making random turns in the forest with no clear destination.

It was getting on towards suppertime when Keeris gave Tristin a sharp jab in the side and motioned for him to look up. If it weren't for Keeris pointing it out to him, Tristin would have simply walked on and never have noticed the large city built in the treetops.

The leader of the small caravan called out to a couple of the colivien standing guard. "You two! Show these prisoners to their cells and inform Milady Shralus that I have returned and seek her council."

"Of course, right away, Sir Jarken" The guards immediately followed their orders without hesitation and started straight for the prisoners.

Tristin and Keeris were ushered into a small cage near the base of the tree and were huddled together with the guards. Almost instantly the cage was lifted from the ground and began to ascend up into the colivien village.

As soon as the cage had reached the treetops, the guards, using spears for persuasion, forced their prisoners into a small building secluded from the rest of the village. Although Tristin was deathly afraid of his current situation, he would have really liked to look around the village. He was captivated by the sight of a whole community that could reside within the tops of the trees.

As the four entered the jailhouse one of the escort guards whistled over to another colivien, who was sitting behind a desk. Without even a glance in their direction he threw a key ring over to one of the guards and simply kept on reading. With that the guards pushed the two prisoners into a large cell, locked the prison door, returned the key and left.

Tristin noticed that Keeris' immense eyes were bouncing around the room, taking in everything, most likely along with any possible means of escape. Unfortunately, the long and strenuous hike through the forest had taken every last ounce of Tristin's energy. Without giving it another thought, he walked silently over to a bed, let his body fall lifelessly down, and at about the same moment drifted off to sleep.

Chapter 11

An Audience with the Queen

Once again, the sun had returned and again filled the forest with its light. Thin bands of the morning sun began penetrating through the bars of the prison window and struck Tristin's face. Slowly he awoke, shaking away the final shreds of fatigue that the previous day had plagued upon him. Keeris, who had finally let his weariness overtake him, fell asleep only a few hours prior after trying to stay awake during the night to protect himself and his new friend.

Only moments after Tristin had awoken did he hear the voices of several colivien heading towards the prison. It was the same two guards who had escorted them to their cell. Then one of the two came forward, unlocked the cell door and, after waking up Keeris, began to speak.

"Alright listen up! You two will follow me, you have your hearing with Milady Shralus who will decide your fate." The guard lifted and broadened his shoulders trying to give himself a more intimidating look as he continued. "When we reach the citadel, you are to use proper manners and ONLY address our queen as milady, and only when first spoken to. Remember, this is your only chance for a good impression before your sentencing so I would advise you make it count."

With that said, the guard pointed a spear in Tristin's face and motioned for the both of them to leave the cell and follow the other guard.

If nothing else, Tristin was pleased to get his wish to see the city. It was truly a treat for the both of them; if the situation had been different both Tristin and Keeris would have loved a proper tour. It seemed that all the treetop paths led toward the center of the city, which also happened to be the location of the citadel. The citadel was a gigantic building and was beautifully constructed. Tristin couldn't quite understand what was holding the whole city up.

Two guards were posted at the front door of

the citadel and immediately gave passage when they saw the accompanied prisoners. The citadel itself seemed even larger from the inside. After walking through numerous rooms and climbing many flights of stairs, the four finally reached the throne room, which was the most beautiful room that Tristin had ever seen. Large stained windows that stretched from the floor to the ceiling turned the suns light into a dazzling display of every color imaginable. At the back of the room were tiered steps that led to the throne itself, and sitting there was Milady Shralus. Shralus was indeed a colivien by size and stature, however, she lacked the intense facial hair which had plagued the male colivien. This made it possible for the captives to truly make out the coliviens features which were just as fair as the elves.

Tristin and Keeris waited at the bottom of the stairs for quite some time as Shralus examined the two of them over and over. The two couldn't decide if she was secretly interrogating them without their knowledge or simply letting them stress over their situation. Finally, she spoke to them, "So, you must be the two whom I have heard so much about this morning. There has been one troubling question that has been greatly puzzling me since I learned that one of my two prisoners happened to be a grimp. Tell me grimp, why have you left the sanctity of your village to trespass in mine?"

Tristin's whole body was sweating with fear. When he and Keeris were caught in the forest by Sir Jarken he seemed to know who Heretius was. Now the only question was, did Heretius leave a good impression with the colivien or a bad one? Tristin didn't have time to think up a proper excuse so he was going to try and keep everything as vague as possible, hoping to avoid any worse punishment than what was already in store for him. However, before he had the chance to begin his tale he was interrupted when Sir Jarken walked into the room and immediately began addressing the queen.

"Milady, I apologize for my absence, I had much more pressing matters which had to be dealt with first." After waiting for the queen's gesture of approval, Jarken continued. "We have........." Jarken abruptly stopped in mid-sentence, looked around the room at the many listening ears, and swiftly walked up the stairs to the queen's side and whispered the rest of his news to the queen so no one else in the room could overhear.

After a few moments, Jarken finished his conversation and waited for the queen's reply. "Very well, we will adhere to that matter after we have finished with the one at hand."

"Very well, milady." Jarken remained at the queen's side looking somewhat distraught, however Tristin had no time to contemplate that matter as the queen again addressed him.

"I apologize for the interruption. We will now continue with your sentencing. It was brought to my attention shortly after you were brought here that you are, in some way or another, an acquaintance to a grimp who goes by the name of Heretius, is this so?"

"Yes milady, it is so." Tristin wished that Heretius could be here with him now, it would make him much more comfortable knowing he had a wizard to protect him.

"My young grimp, to make this somewhat easier on yourself, rest assured that I am already aware of the reason you have left your homeland. Although, I may not be familiar with many of the minor details which led you here. You see, the name Heretius is anything but a foreign word amongst us colivien, as well as the acts of the grimps of the past."

Gaining a small bit of courage Tristin decided to cut in. "Ummm, milady, excuse the interruption, but would you call these acts that my grandparents and ancestors committed decent or indecent acts?"

A thin smile found its way upon Shralus' face

as she rose and walked down the steps towards Tristin. "I can see that our lack of hospitality has caused you to presume the worst repercussions from each of my questions. Well, let it be known that the deeds of which I spoke were all, for the most part, respectable and with the best of intentions. Yet, all of this can wait for now, why don't you and I, along with Sir Jarken and your friend, retire to the dining room for some breakfast."

The thought of food made Tristin's mouth water, he hadn't eaten since stopping for lunch the previous day and even that was much less than he was accustomed to back home. The four walked into the dining room to find that the large banquet table had already been set along with four placements of dishes and silverware.

Taking their cue from the queen, Jarken, Tristin, and Keeris sat down at the table. Since there was only the four of them sitting at a table that used to serve a hundred guests at a time, they sat together at the end of the table with the queen taking her accustomed seat at the head.

The queen gave both her guests some time to savor their breakfast. As she had mentioned earlier, she didn't truly know how hard their journey had been and wanted to let them regain their strength. Shralus waited until the maid had taken their finished plates away until she resumed the conversation.

"I apologize, we've never been properly introduced. My name is Queen Shralus, but everyone around here simply calls me milady, and you are already familiar with Sir Jarken being as he is the real reason you are here."

Taking his cue, Tristin continued the introduction. "My name is Tristin, and this is my friend Keeris, of the Pleeris Valley."

"Well, I must say, it is a pleasure to meet with you both, unfortunate it can't be due to circumstances of a cheerier nature. As I said earlier, I know the reason Heretius sent you. The Great War affected every race quite dramatically and we are all very well aware of recent events. Still, I would like to hear a little of your tale if you would be so kind to amuse me with your story."

Tristin blushed slightly at the mention of his journey through the forest being a tale worth hearing. Still, he was anxious to find out more about the colivien so trading information sounded like a good idea. "Well, first of all, I do have something I need to confess. I was never sent by Heretius. You see it was actually my best friend Darius who was chosen for this quest, I simply left my village to find my friend and lend what help I could."

Shralus and Jarken exchanged glances, they seemed quite unsure as how to take this news. Jarken, being more interested in the one truly sent interrupted Tristin. "Tell me this Tristin, what happened to Darius?"

"I only wish I knew. I lost his trail at Windover Pond, a three-day journey outside my village. However, I did come across his pack, which contained everything he needed for his quest. It was then that I decided to take on his burden and do my best in completing his quest for him."

Shralus was still puzzled by the story and also broke in to question Tristin. "Before you continue, if you would be so kind as to help clear up a matter for me. How is it that you are familiar with your friend's quest since it was all to be kept a great secret? Also, what chances do you believe you have against a dragon?"

"Well, to answer your first question, Darius and I were the best of friends and there is no secret large enough to keep between us. Also, Heretius never attempted to keep any information from me, he even allowed me to participate in Darius' magical practices. And, well, to answer your second question, nothing has ever frightened me more than the thought of not only leaving everyone I know and love, but to risk near-certain death by doing so. Nevertheless, Darius is my friend and I could never let him tackle anything this large without doing everything I possibly could to help, and I know he would have done the same for me. Also, since I lost him to the forest, I wasn't really left with any other suitable options since there was no way I could go home without him and I couldn't just give up."

Tristin paused for a moment to clear a lump that had caught in the back of his throat. Although he still held onto hope that his friend was alive, a nagging feeling in the pit of his stomach told him otherwise. Shralus could see Tristin was visibly shaken and personally poured a glass of water for the grief-stricken grimp. After a short silence, Tristin went on with his tale. It was nearly lunchtime when Tristin finished his story and all the questions that he was capable of answering were answered.

After the long morning, the queen rose from her seat and addressed her guest. "I thank you for joining me for breakfast and once again I apologize for my antics of last night, tonight you will have a proper place to sleep. As for now, I have other very pressing matters that need my immediate attention. If it would please you, Captain Jarken will show you around our city, and I would very much like to continue this conversation over supper this afternoon. At that point, we will decide upon a few pressing details concerning your journey and see what help we can possibly aid you. Till then, I pray you enjoy my city and I will see the three of you later." With that said the queen left the table and disappeared through one of the side doors of the dining room.

"Well my young friends, I guess that gives us the rest of the day to do as you please. However, I would first like to take this opportunity to offer my humblest of apologies in respect to last night. Now, to get things started let's give you the proper tour of the city."

Tristin and Keeris were very excited to finally see the city without the fear of death hovering over their shoulders. The two spent the rest of the day walking through the village with Jarken, wandering through the shops and trying an assortment of exotic foods. In the time they were together both Tristin and Keeris also became quite good friends with Jarken as he showed them the highlights of the city. The other colivien of the city were also very excited at the sight of a foreigner, which had become extremely rare in recent years.

The day had gone by far faster than Tristin or Keeris could possibly have hoped, and it was quickly nearing suppertime and their prior engagement with the queen. After following the roads through the city and again finding their way to the citadel, the three decided it was time to join the queen for supper and determine what was to be done concerning the remainder of Tristin's journey.

Once again, the guards seeing the familiar face of Sir Jarken and his prisoners bowed slightly and let the three enter. Before entering back into the dining room Jarken stopped Tristin and Keeris. "Listen, my new friends, I don't really know what will happen after we enter this room and even more so after you both depart from our city but I can tell you this. Much will change, and quite rapidly, in the coming days. I don't know if I will ever see you again after tomorrow so I want to wish you a safe trip and I also have a small token to give you tomorrow before you depart. But for now, let us have dinner with the queen and hope for the best."

Chapter 12

The Stranger Returns

As Tristin, Keeris, and Sir Jarken entered the dining room they found that they wouldn't be dining alone with Shralus as they did earlier that morning. Not only were there a couple high ranking delegates of the colivien village, but joining them also were two creatures clad entirely in green of which Tristin immediately recognized as elves. Taken slightly by surprise at the audience, the three hesitated slightly before taking their reserved seats at the table.

The room began to fill with chatter as the different delegates began discussing current affairs amongst each other. Many trivial issues were discussed between the colivien and the elves as they waited. It seemed to Tristin that hours had passed as he listened in on the many discussions around the table. He was unexpectedly startled as a very fidgety Sir Jarken popped out of his chair to salute his queen as she entered the room. The others all mimicked Jarken's actions out of respect for milady Shralus, who gracefully bowed and bid them all take their seats.

Tristin had hoped that the discussion would have followed in the same fashion as it had at breakfast, however it seemed all of the other members in the room were quite anxious to begin. Once the queen had sat, she was immediately followed by a dozen attendants who quickly filled the table with a delicious looking meal. Unfortunately, before Tristin could pick up his fork and take his first bite an argument had broken out, and it seemed the issue they were arguing about was him!

Tristin seemed to have the support of both Jarken and the queen, but the elves were convinced he would fail and bring disaster upon them all. The discussion quickly got out of hand, despite the queen's efforts to calm it down. Tristin didn't hear what was said, but it was enough to provoke the two elves to shoot straight from their chair and begin hurling insults at everyone in their native language. Shralus lowered her head in failure, she had hoped she could have prevented the discussion from getting out of control but it was too much for her.

Tristin gave a frightful look to Keeris who had slouched low in his chair, ready to defend himself, which seemed like it may be necessary, and would have been if not for a silent guest. Just as the argument was about to turn into a physical battle, a cloaked figure whom Tristin had just noticed for the first time, stood. Silently he rose his hand into the air which created a dark cloud above the dinner table. A moment later a blinding bolt of lightning flashed between the arguing sides throwing both the elves and the colivien back into their seats. The massive dining table was now split in two as order was once again brought back to the room which was now completely silent. The attention of the room was turned fully to the cloaked figure as it seemed that Tristin wasn't the only one surprised to see him standing there.

The cloak served its purpose well; no one was able to make out any physical features hidden under the hood. The cloaked creature slowly scanned the room, stopping at each of the guests, staring deeply into them. After a long and unpleasant silence, the cloaked figure spoke in a low and powerful voice.

"Fools! I had hoped that you would have

learned from the mistakes of your ancestors. It's a shame that it takes more than the threat of extinction to change your attitudes. You all know why you have been gathered in this room, and you also all know what needs to be done, so why complicate matters? You my friend," the cloaked figure continued while pointing a finger towards Tristin. "You seem to have quickly grown in popularity, unfortunately not to everyone's liking. From what I've gathered from the debate this is not the same grimp chosen by Heretius to help in freeing us from the red dragon. However, it also would appear that at no time did Heretius not choose this grimp for the task, if you understand my saying. All here know of Heretius, along with that, his deeds and promise to us all. So then, why not put that same trust in our young friend here. Beyond the discussion at hand, we are all plagued by many other problems, each of which are all much closer to home and might be requiring our near immediate attention. Now then, I would recommend you take the advice of a stranger and let those whom the path has chosen follow that path, for those who hinder its course may find their own to become much more difficult. Now then, finish your debate in a civilized manner and focus only on the large issues, otherwise you will come to no agreement at all."

After he stopped speaking the cloaked figure

left the table and vanished out the side door of the room. Then, after another extended period of silence the debate continued once again.

Sir Jarken took the opportunity to make his voice heard while the others were still slightly shocked by their unknown guest. "My friends, I believe that the words spoken by our mysterious guest are ones we should abide by. Why not let our young friend here continue the journey that was so unexpectedly thrown upon him. In the meantime, I think we all need to prepare for the worst... We need to prepare our people for another great war."

There wasn't really anything else that needed saying, so with a simple nod of their heads the other delegates agreed. Not another word was spoken through the meal until dessert had been served. One of the elves began speaking with his eyes fixed upon Jarken.

"I would deem that both your suggestion as well as that of our cloaked friend be justly noted. However, I disagree partly with your proposal to ready our own people for war. I feel that we would all be much better off if we were to combine our forces along with our skills immediately, so we might crush any uprising before it gets out of hand."

Queen Shralus was pleased that they were

finally able to settle the matter in a civilized manner, and agreed with the elf's suggestion. Dinner was quickly wrapped up after that and Sir Jarken kindly escorted Tristin and Keeris to their bedchambers.

"My friends, I will be leaving you for the rest of the evening. I will be continuing our debate with the elves and finalizing our peace treaty and merger of our armies. You will have free reign of the city if it would please you, or you may stay here and rest before you return to your journey, that choice is yours. Goodnight, I will see you off tomorrow." Jarken then left the room and Keeris and Tristin were alone.

"Well," Keeris slowly wandered around the room admiring the decorations as he spoke. "This has really turned out to be quite an odd last few days wouldn't you say, wouldn't you say? I mean I was just minding my own business, business, lazily walking around the forest when I run into this strange guy, get captured and brought to a hidden colivien city, and now I'm actually considering finding and, oh yes! Attacking a dragon, mmhhmmm!?"

Tristin felt his heart drop, he had never forced Keeris to follow him, actually he had never even invited him to come along. But now, the thought of having to continue on alone through the forest seemed even harder than it had the first time.

"Umm,,, you know you don't have to come along with me if you don't want. I mean, it will be dangerous and you..."

"Are you kidding, kidding!" Keeris's face lit up with a smile. "There's no way, no way I'm letting you finish this thing alone. I've had more fun in the past two days than I have in the past two years, and it's not like you couldn't use my help, my help, when I found you, you were hiding from the trees, mmhhmmm!"

Tristin let himself fall on his bed laughing with Keeris, he was relieved to know he would have a friend to follow him.

There wasn't much else that needed to be said between the two. It was getting late and knowing that they would have a long day ahead of them they decided to get some sleep.

Tristin laid in his bed staring at the ceiling, which he noticed for the first time was covered entirely in glass allowing him to see the star-filled sky. As he stared into the emptiness of space Tristin was constantly reminded of his best friend who was out there somewhere, all alone. While thinking about Darius, Tristin's thoughts kept switching back towards Keeris who had filled the void of friendship that Darius had left upon leaving both him and the village behind to embark on Heretius's quest.

More thoughts of Darius, his home, and all the things that he left behind began swarming through Tristin's head. However, the weight of sleep was taking its toll on him once again as he slowly began dozing off. Just as he was about to close his eyes for the last time that night and drift off into a revitalizing slumber, he noticed a small shadow flash across the room.

In an instant, the drowsiness was flushed from his eyes as he quickly scanned the room in a panic. Tristin desperately wanted to get Keeris's attention, but he was facing the opposite direction and Tristin didn't want to let the intruder know he was awake and knew of his presence.

Tristin kept searching the room, slowly getting the nerve to sit up and get a better view of his surroundings. Perhaps it was just his imagination or maybe just a bird flying over the window in the ceiling, but whatever it was it didn't appear to still be in the room. Tristin decided it was a false alarm and didn't want to wake up Keeris so he turned towards the wall, and laid back down to sleep.

There it was again! As Tristin turned his head to make himself more comfortable, he saw a pitch-black figure standing at his bedside. He wanted to scream, he tried to scream, but nothing would come out. Tristin was frozen with fear and couldn't even defend himself from the impostor. He could feel the screams building up inside his throat, trying to break past some impenetrable barrier. If only he could signal Keeris, or do anything other than stare straight into the blackness. Tristin watched as a hand emerged from within the cloak of the figure and slowly moved towards him. Tristin felt his whole body go limp, when the hand touched him it was as if all the distress and terror that was bottled up inside him had suddenly vanished. He was now free to move and speak but the urge had seemed to fade with the fear. The same hand that had touched him moved from his shoulder and pointed towards the door. The creature then turned and left the room.

Tristin felt unusually relaxed, it was as if everything had suddenly become clear and the questions Tristin didn't even realize he had, were suddenly answered. An abrupt thirst for knowledge drove him to leave his room and follow the cloaked figure in search of more answers.

As Tristin exited his room, he immediately noticed his cloaked acquaintance waiting for him down the hall. Once the black creature took notice that Tristin had begun to follow him, he began to lead Tristin through numerous stairwells and hallways until they came to their destination. It was a library, never before had Tristin seen so many books all gathered into the same room. They were standing in a large round room and the walls were literally covered with books. Looking up Tristin saw that there were three other levels just like this one and a large spiral staircase connecting them all. It was wonderful! He could have spent hours on one floor of this library searching through all the books. However, Tristin's attention was returned to the cloaked figure who was ushering him towards two chairs that were placed in front of an enormous fireplace, probably intended as a place to sit and read.

The two made themselves comfortable in the large chairs as Tristin's host waved his hand in front of the barren fireplace, creating a fire that instantly warmed the room. As the two sat staring into the fire the cloaked figure was taken by surprise when Tristin decided to initiate the conversation.

"We've met before, haven't we?" Tristin's eyes never left the fire as he continued. "You're the one I met with before I left my village. A couple of times I thought I knew who you were, but then you seemed wholly different, as if there's more than one of you hiding beneath that cloak. So, have you decided it was time to tell me why you're following me? Or is that another secret that will have to wait?"

The cloaked figure smiled slightly and just as Tristin his eyes never left the fire when he spoke. "Yes, my friend, there are many things which I hoped to reveal to both you and Darius on this night. Unfortunately, we seem to be missing your friend, do you know what has become of him?"

"No, not entirely. All I know is that something terrible must have happened to him near Windover Pond. It was at the bank of the pond that I found his pack and all the items he took with him before he left. I had hoped he had escaped from whatever evils had caused him to leave behind his belongings and that I might catch up with him further along the path. But now all that seems like a dream, and I don't think I will ever see Darius again." Tristin dropped his head into his hands and his breaths started coming in faster, heavier burst as he remembered his lost friend.

"Keep your chin up little one, you should never lose hope, especially when there is so little to base it on. You see, long ago there were seven gateways leading to the Dark Realm. Each of these was hidden throughout the land and all have been sealed off by distinct natural landmarks. Now your friend Darius, he disappeared right on top of one of them, the one known as the Windover Portal. Although these doorways are quite well hidden, I've been informed Darius is in possession of the Talisman of Odigin which is a magical amulet that reveals pathways to its holder, whether he realizes it or not. I would assume that Darius stumbled across the portal entrance and is now, or at least was at the time, somewhere in either the Tunnels of Bhulek or quite possibly the Dark Realm itself!"

"The tunnels of what? I've heard of the Dark Realm, but where is this other place?"

"The Tunnels of Bhulek is a maze of dark and musty underground passageways that connects Trubanius and Broudiun. Unfortunately, the caverns are now overflowing with orcs. The problem with orcs is that they are always in groups. You see if you can get one alone it shouldn't prove too hard a task to defeat it since they are unintelligent and clumsy. However, once you get three or four of them together, they are strong enough that even an experienced wizard may have problems disposing of them. So, don't fear that your friend has lost his way, because never was he given a path to follow to his destination. As to Darius' safety, I wouldn't recommend running off in search of him. You should know better than anyone the pleasure of traveling with a companion, however don't let that distract you from the quest you took upon yourself after you thought you lost Darius."

"So then… do you know that he is still alive?" Tristin, for the first time since leaving Windover Pond, felt hope for Darius.

"No," the cloaked creature lifted his gaze from the fire and tilted his head towards Tristin. "Regrettably, I know no more than you regarding the well-being and ware bouts of your friend. Nevertheless, you may find it somewhat comforting to hear the Tunnels of Bhulek is the home to more than simply orcs. Darius has an equal chance of crossing paths with as many creatures that would befriend him as would destroy him, so never give up hope."

The two sat in silence for nearly an hour collecting their thoughts, trying to find the right words to express themselves. It was nearing midnight and the day's activities had drained Tristin's energy.

The cloaked figure appeared to take notice of Tristin's fatigue and resumed the conversation. "My young friend, I have decided that it isn't quite time to reveal my identity to you. I would strongly advise that you try your best to finish the quest that you took upon yourself, without worrying yourself about the past. Until we meet again, I would like to give you another small bit of advice. First of all, let no one else know of the purpose of your travels. Trust is a great thing, but can also be extremely dangerous if it isn't returned. Second..." the cloaked figure rose from his chair and disappeared into the darkness of the library. Tristin could hear his footsteps as he climbed up the spiral staircase. After the sound had faded Tristin could make out a faint glow coming from the third floor of the library, and then noticed his mysterious friend return to the staircase. After waiting again for the sound of footsteps to cease, Tristin again saw the cloaked creature standing alongside him, arms extended, handing him a book. "Here, this is something that may help you finish this journey of yours, and hopefully increase your chances of success. Well, I suppose this is goodbye again little grimp. Take care and look after Keeris, a companion through the forest may be of more usefulness than any magic or advice I could offer."

Again, the figure disappeared into the darkness, only this time Tristin knew he wouldn't be seeing or hearing him again, or at least anytime soon. With that, he to decided it was time to end the night and slowly dragged his weary body back to his room and upon hitting his bed fell instantly into a deep, dream filled sleep.

Chapter 13

Onward to the Swamps

Tristin slowly opened his eyes as the blurred room slowly came into focus. Keeris looked as if he had been up for quite some time and Tristin could tell by the height of the sun through the window that it was already late in the morning.

"Well it's about time you woke up, woke up. I think they're all waiting for us outside the citadel to see us off, mmhhmmm."

Tristin immediately jumped from his bed and began collecting his things. Apparently, his talk with the cloaked figure went further into the night than he had realized and caused him to oversleep. "How long have they been waiting for us?"

"Well, well, Sir Jarken has been in here three times now to see if you'd woken, but every time he refuses to let me or anyone else wake you. He says he wants you to get a good and full night's sleep, night's sleep, since it may be your last in a while."

"Well it's nice to hear that he's optimistic about all this. Come on, let's get going, we've got a long couple days ahead of us." Tristin motioned Keeris to follow by nodding his head and walked out the door.

The palace seemed very empty considering it was already midmorning, and the two travelers were soon to find out why. When they reached the front doors of the citadel the two now familiar guards opened the door and bid them farewell. Before either of them could take one step outside the palace doors, Captain Jarken, who had behind him what appeared to be the entire colivien city, immediately confronted them.

"I told you that I would be here to see you off, and I also told you that I had something for you." With a quick wink, Sir Jarken turned and ushered Tristin and Keeris down past the gathered crowd.

Tristin and Keeris were amazed at the number of colivien who lived in the city, they had wandered around the day before but hadn't seen any of the dwelling areas. Sir Jarken proudly escorted the two through the crowd until they reached Queen Shralus who was waiting for them near the edge of the city.

"Welcome, welcome!" Shralus seemed to be in an exceptionally good mood as she greeted her guests. "I deeply wish you could stay here with us longer, however these times call for an unfortunate haste. Because of the necessity of speed on your quest we wish to offer our assistance to help you reach the swamps many times faster than your feet could ever carry you. My small friends, I would deeply………"

As the queen was speaking there was a sudden gasp that flowed through the crowd as each of the colivien took a step backwards. Tristin and Keeris were instantly gripped with fear as they saw a giant creature rise up behind the queen.

Two large and scaly wings beat gusts of wind down on the colivien and their guests. Its head alone was twice the size of Tristin, and its enormous fangs were the size of his fists. The creature was immediately recognized by everyone as one of the legendary dragons. As the dragon landed on the platform it raised its head into the air, gave out an ear-piercing roar while spitting fire high through the treetops.

Tristin and Keeris didn't want to wait around and see what else the dragon was capable of and quickly turned to run. However, they weren't able to get more than two steps away before crashing headlong into Sir Jarken who hadn't flinched at the dragon's arrival. Tristin jumped back to his feet, hid behind Jarken, and began surveying the situation. Although the colivien had taken a step back at the dragon's appearance, they too, like Sir Jarken didn't seem the least bit concerned. The queen chuckled at her guest's reaction but quickly regained her composure and walked over towards Keeris and Tristin.

"Friends, I am truly very sorry about this whole ordeal. I would have liked to inform you about the arrival of Erquein however, I myself wasn't aware of his visit until earlier this morning. Apparently, this was a surprise arranged by Captain Jarken to assist you in the remainder of your quest."

"Umm, milady?" Keeris was still having some trouble controlling himself after the terrible scare the dragon had given him. "How, how exactly is this, err, Erquein, going to help, help us?"

"Well Mr. Keeris, Erquein has agreed to fly you to your destination."

Keeris and Tristin exchanged a nervous

glance. Although Tristin did recall throughout Heretius's numerous stories that there were good dragons in existence, the simple fact that this was indeed a dragon in front of him worried them both. Erquein wasn't helping matters either. After hearing the nervous tone of Keeris' voice, he turned his neck to position his head within three feet of Keeris. Although very intimidating, the dragon was actually quite beautiful to look at. The scales that covered Erquein's body changed colors as the sun reflected off at different angles, so at times he donned a golden yellow armor and when he shifted his body it changed to a sleek dark-silver. Luckily for the three would-be companions, Jarken immediately stepped in to prevent any bad blood from arising between them.

"I believe none of you have been properly introduced. Tristin, Keeris, this is Erquein, he has willingly agreed to assist you on your quest." Jarken continued while patting Erquein on the side of his head. "And Erquein, these are the two travelers of which I spoke of earlier, they are Tristin and Keeris. These are the ones sent to help save us from Drelokh."

Erquein again turned his attention to Keeris and Tristin and when he spoke his low and powerful voice sounded as if it echoed inside his throat. "Well then my new friends, if we're headed towards the swamps, I would advise we leave as soon as possible. Quickly speak your farewells and any questions or concerns you may have they can be addressed along the way."

Tristin, although still greatly intimidated by the dragon, agreed fully with Erquein and was also in a great hurry to resume his journey. So, following the dragon's wishes, Tristin and Keeris quickly thanked Shralus and Jarken for their hospitality and returned to Erquein.

Erquein had been fitted with a saddle, which contained two padded leather seats which had been attached on his back, directly behind his neck. The saddle was a perfect fit for Tristin and Keeris as they hurriedly got themselves and their things settled. With a mighty flap of his wings Erquein lifted off the ground and within seconds had risen high above the treetops. As the three companions began their journey together, they could faintly hear the voice of Jarken calling out to them.

"Take care my friends! Until we meet again."

Nothing could have prepared Tristin or Keeris for the beauty and tranquility of the world from the back of a dragon. Erquein slowly flapped his wings as he soared with the wind currents. Keeris was watching the ground below them move by at speeds much faster than himself or Tristin could have ever traveled.

Keeris seemed to warm up to the idea of befriending a dragon faster than Tristin as he engaged in conversation. "Erquein, I just, just wanted, wanted to thank you for your help, it's amazing how much faster one can travel by air!"

To the surprise of both Tristin and Keeris, Erquein bent his neck around to face the two while he spoke and at the same time was able to fly perfectly straight.

"It's my pleasure little ones. You must both be extremely powerful wizards if you plan on taking on Drelokh."

"Well no not really, that is why we have to first stop in the swamps so that I can learn more powerful magic. There's someone there who will hopefully be able to help me acquire the knowledge I'll need to defeat the Red Dragon. Oh, and who is this Drelokh, is he another evil dragon?"

Tristin and Keeris could feel Erquein's body shudder slightly as he let out a low chuckle. "No, my friend, and luckily enough for you since you're still an amateur magician. Drelokh is the Red Dragon's true name, it was the name he was given at birth before choosing the path of evil and greed. You'll find in time that there is great power in knowing one's true name. As for Drelokh, he lost his name when he began his path of destruction, I would surmount that he no longer has any knowledge of that name. Nevertheless, it makes no difference now since all his followers, with the exception of one, are too frightened to ever speak directly to him."

Keeris appeared to be hanging on the dragons every word as he listened to the story. "Why did Drelokh lose his name?"

Erquein was pleased to not only have the company but also the questions since he nearly always traveled alone. Well, you see Keeris, a dragon is neither good nor evil like all the other creatures of the world, so that makes it fairly hard to explain. When a dragon denies himself and goes against his own true nature, which is also the heart of a dragon's existence, he rejects his own being and loses his true identity. Unfortunately, it's something that a dragon feels and can't really be described with any accuracy. The best definition I can give you would be this, a dragon's name is like his soul; if a dragon chooses to reject his name it alters his trueness as a dragon. Now in Drelokhs case, he denied himself in order to gain power, which was not one of the traits he was born with and also not a part of his name."

Tristin's mind was racing with questions and

he interrupted the dragon without realizing he was speaking out loud. "So, if Drelokh can give up his name to gain power doesn't he also have to lose something in the process?"

"Ahhh, a very wise question young grimp. Yes, Drelokh gave up his greatest strength when he denied his name. That was the main reason for his downfall all those years ago, and if you're to defeat him it will also be the cause for his final demise. Unfortunately, only the dragon that lost his true power and strength can tell you what that power was, and that is the riddle you must decipher if you are to destroy him."

Keeris nearly fell out of his seat as he soaked in every word Erquein told them. "So, could you could you tell us what your true power is?"

Erquein straightened his neck back out to watch where he was flying as he spoke. "No, I can't tell you that. There are only two ways for a dragon to learn what his true power is, and that is by either losing it as Drelokh did, or through some great and unselfish deed. So I..."

Without giving his passengers any warning Erquein fell silent and went into a dive, hurtling himself along with Keeris and Tristin straight for the ground. As the blood rushed to their heads Keeris and Tristin blacked out and when they regained consciousness they were hidden under the thick branches of the forest.

Tristin and Keeris stared wide-eyed at one another as they turned their attention back towards Erquein and spoke together. "What did you do that for?"

Erquein lowered his voice to a whisper as he bent his neck to once again face his companions. "We must be nearing the borders of the swamps, there were four griffins' just ahead, luckily they didn't spot us."

"Hold on," Tristin was becoming confused once again. "I was under the impression that the griffins were good, so why are we hiding?"

"Tristin if you want to survive this quest of yours there is something very important you must understand. There is no such thing as a purely good or evil race, all creatures no matter how foul or noble all have their assortments of good and evil, many have just learned to keep their true feelings hidden under a shroud of misdirection. For example, not all grimps are good, even your own race has been littered with evil and mistrust. And even more so like myself, you were under the impression that all dragons were the ultimate in malevolent creatures until you met me.

Enough of that talk for now though, I think we should stay here until dusk and then once the griffins have left we can make for this house in the swamps, it shouldn't be too far off now."

After making up his mind, Erquein laid his head down and fell asleep as Keeris and Tristin made themselves comfortable and sat down for lunch.

Chapter 14

Theshius's Secret

Not long after Tristin and Keeris had finished their lunch did they lay down for a short mid-day nap. Tristin had felt as if he had just closed his eyes when he felt the large and powerful claw of Erquein vigorously shaking his whole body trying to wake him up. As Tristin rubbed the sleep away from his eyes, he was surprised to see that the sun was already half-covered by the horizon, and night would quickly be upon them.

"Well my little friends, I think it is time we leave." Erquein lowered his body so that Keeris and Tristin could climb onto his back.

With a powerful flap of his wings, Erquein's body shot into the air and above the treetops. Tristin and Keeris immediately began scanning the horizon for any sight of the large griffins. Erquein then made the gap between them and the swamps disappear with a great swiftness as the last shards of sunlight slowly fell behind the horizon and were replaced by the darkness of night. Luckily enough for Tristin and Keeris, the light reflecting off the moon was more than adequate to light the way for Erquein, since dragons have the ability to dilate their eyes collecting more light than most creatures, he would have no issues traveling in the night.

The world looked quite different from the sky at night than it had that morning. Everything seemed still as if the whole forest had died with the sunlight, waiting for its return before life could resume. Then there were the rivers which could be spotted rather easily as they reflected the moonlight, looking much like shining roads cutting randomly throughout the forest. However, the landscape began to change rather abruptly as Erquein passed beyond the forest. The vegetation quickly died away and was replaced by deceased and leafless trees while the remainder of the landscape was covered by swamp water.

The swamp of Kilvay was a slimy, insect-ridden sea that enveloped anyone and anything that dared step foot in its appalling waters. Tristin was very grateful that he had Erquein to fly them over the deathtrap; he wasn't quite sure how he and Keeris would have crossed that godforsaken place on foot.

It seemed Erquein was also slightly curious about their apparent destination as he turned his head to face his passengers. "Why do you suppose anyone would voluntarily live in such a desolate place? Unless this friend of yours has sprouted wings, it would seem as if this house we're searching for is more of a prison. And while I'm on the subject of this house, might you happen to know where it's located?"

"Unfortunately, Erquein I don't know the proper answers to either of your questions. I have a map that shows the general vicinity of the house, but regrettably, it isn't very detailed."

Keeris seemed to be having some difficulty staying in his seat as he tried to join in the conversation. "Perhaps, yes perhaps the house wouldn't be all too well concealed since there's no vegetation to hide it. So, it can't be all that hard to find... can it, mmhhmmm?"

Keeris was right, the home of Theshius was by no means hidden. However, it wasn't quite what the three of them were looking for. Amidst some deeper swamp waters was a tree that although was exceptionally larger than the rest, looked no different. If it hadn't been for a steady stream of smoke emitting from the top of a larger tree branch, they would have simply passed over not giving the tree a second thought.

"Well would you look at that, I believe this tree has a chimney!" Erquein gave out a short billowy laugh at the odd sight.

With a soundless dive, the dragon and his companions quickly reached the ground outside the tree, which was moderately hard when compared to the rest of the swamp. They had found what they were looking for, directly in the side of the tree was a door and to its side was a small glass window.

"Well, I believe this is where our paths part my small friends. A great war is brewing and my services are greatly needed in the colivien city, so I must quickly return to them. However, I wouldn't be too surprised if we were to cross paths again before this war has come to an end. So, till then my friends, may your journey lead you both to the greatness your lives deserve." Once again Erquein flapped his mighty wings and lifted his body into the sky.

Tristin and Keeris watched as Erquein's body

grew smaller and smaller until it disappeared into the darkness. Tristin felt a strange feeling fill his body as he realized that the half of his quest he was aware of had just come to an end. The door to Theshius' home lay merely an arm's length away. What answers would he find here and how many more questions would he discover in the process?

"Well, I suppose we should knock?" Tristin wasn't sure why he was so nervous to finally meet Theshius. He knew she was supposed to help on their quest, but he couldn't keep from reminding himself of who was really supposed to be standing in front of this door. This path was chosen for Darius. However, he had lost his friend back at Windover Pond and along with that a piece of himself. But for now, he would have to put all that behind him. So, with a deep breath, Tristin moved towards the house and knocked firmly on the door.

Tristin had barely pulled his hand back before the door swung open revealing a short, cloaked figure that filled the doorway.

The cloaked figure tilted her head slightly and spoke with a soft and soothing female voice. "Ahhh, Tristin, Keeris, I have been expecting you for some time now. Please, please come in and make yourselves comfortable."

"Wait!" Tristin glanced over at Keeris who had raised an eyebrow and simply shrugged his shoulders. "How do you know our names?"

The cloaked woman slowly turned back to face her guest, "well I suppose we could discuss that all here; however, I believe that may turn into somewhat of a long conversation and I don't think it would be either wise or comfortable to have it standing at my front door."

With a silent nod of approval Tristin and Keeris followed their host into her home. Tristin wasn't sure what to expect as he passed through the doorway. Although the homes of grimps were built into the stumps of trees, their house was also built into the ground around it. However, the fact that this tree was located in a swamp made bringing in dirt or digging down somewhat impossible. Theshius' home was built in layers, whereas most homes would use hallways to connect each room Theshius used staircases since each room was built on top of the next. Tristin and Keeris followed their host up two flights of stairs, through a kitchen along with a sitting room, until they reached what looked like a library.

Following the natural curvature of the walls was a bookshelf, which wrapped entirely around the room and reached straight to the ceiling. The bookshelf was overflowing with numerous books of many different shapes and sizes. In the center of the room was a large, round wooden table with chairs surrounding it. Hovering over the table was a chandelier which seemed to light itself, as if by magic, the instant the three entered the room. Additionally, placed in front of two of the chairs encircling the table were dinner settings.

"Now, I would assume you are both rather tired and hungry after today's journey, so I propose that first you eat then we will discuss the questions pertaining to your visit." Without the slightest of movements, Theshius filled the table with food and the goblets with drink. "Once you have both eaten your fill I will return. This is now a time of rest for you both, think not of any part of your mission, for now it does not exist." Theshius then turned and followed the stairway back down to one of the lower rooms.

"Well Tristin, I don't suppose we can pass up free food, mmhhmmm."

Keeris made his way over to the table, followed by Tristin, and sat down to eat. "This Theshius friend of yours isn't really what I had in mind had in mind, if it weren't for the fact that you knew her, I would be slightly nervous, nervous by the whole cloak getup."

"Well buddy, I don't want to break your sense of security here, but until now I had never met her before. So, I haven't really known what to expect this whole time either, it's somewhat like the piecing together of a puzzle."

Keeris pulled his goblet away from his mouth and stared at it for a short while. "Then how, how, how do we know exactly that this is really Theshius, I mean anyone could, could be hiding under that cloak, mmhhmmm?"

Tristin ignored Keeris' hesitancy to eat his food. "Well, there are three things that cause me to believe that that was Theshius. First of all, she not only knew our names but also was expecting us, which truthfully worried me slightly since it wasn't either of us who were selected for this mission. However, there is also the fact that this has to be her house. How many other homes do you recall seeing as we flew over the swamps? Finally, even if we are in the wrong home with the wrong host, how would we possibly escape through the swamp? I think Theshius is right and we need to stop worrying about everything and anything while we still can."

Keeris didn't respond to Tristin's theory, he merely nodded, gave Tristin a half-smile and continued eating without another word.

The food was excellent and reminded Tristin of his carefree days' back home. If only he could magically make everything go back to the way it was before any of this started. They were both nearing the end of their meals and Tristin knew that Theshius would again be joining them. However, there was a question that had been troubling him since leaving the colivien city that Tristin wanted to ask while he and Keeris were still alone.

"Keeris, I know I brought this subject up before but many things have changed since then. You know that from here on everything will be very much different and much more difficult. So, I just wanted to tell you that if you don't want to travel any farther than this point, not only is it perfectly fine with me, but it will also make me feel much better knowing that I'm not endangering the lives of anyone else on this journey. There may not likely be a better time for you to turn back so I would suggest doing so as soon as we get out of this swamp."

A large smile appeared on Keeris' face as he looked up to face Tristin, his large eyes reflecting the light of the chandelier. "Now, now I'm pretty sure that I told you I was going to see this through to the end, the end, so you can give up the whole, this is going to be dangerous, routine. Besides, where, where would I go, I couldn't leave knowing the fate of

Trubanius is in YOUR hands. Without me you, you might as well just give up now, yup."

"Well, I see you're both finished, excellent!" This time Theshius returned from the upper level of the house, surprising both Tristin and Keeris. She ignored the dumbfounded look on their faces. With a wave of her hand, she cleared the table and sat down to join them.

"So, I suppose we have quite a lot to talk about, don't we? I think I will chop off a good portion of this conversation and let you in on a little secret. There's not much about your journey that is unknown to me, right down to your friend Darius."

At this point, Tristin was only moderately surprised to hear this but couldn't stop himself from asking. "How is it that you know all about our travels, can you see things that are going on all around the world from here? And if you know that, do you also know where we must go from here?"

"Slow down there young one. We had better make ourselves comfortable because I don't know how long this might take." Theshius stood up and led both Keeris and Tristin to the side of the room which contained three cushioned chairs next to the bookshelves. Once her two guests settled themselves, Theshius then continued.

"First of all, I will let you know a few things pertaining to the real reason you journeyed so far to see me. The real reason Heretius sent you this long way was not simply so that you could pick up some books to learn magic. The truth of the matter is that Heretius may be your best bet if you're looking for a teacher, via verbally or in a book. Regardless, what he may have told you or Darius, he is by no means too old to instruct any in the arts of magic. The actual means for this journey was to give you the real-life experiences you would need before you could rightfully learn the more complicated forms of magic. You see, anyone could sit down and learn all the spells in existence and still lose to someone as knowledgeable as you two are now. True magic, and more importantly powerful magic, comes from the trials one faces throughout his life. These trials and experiences will push you to better understand the magic and its potential, along with your own abilities. This simple reason is why Heretius is known for his great power, his strength comes from his own journeys."

Theshius paused for a short while to let some of this sink in before she began confusing the two of them to the point where they wanted to give up. "Now there are two more things I want to tell you before we begin your study of magic. One, to tell you about the trials you will face once you leave my swamps and also to enlighten you both concerning my knowledge of your quest up to this point.

First of all, and for the moment the most important matter, is that of the remainder of your quest. After you leave here, you will have to travel to the Cliffs of Shemod, from there you will have to seek out a mystical weapon, cursed by an evil spell. From there you will have to seek out Drelokh and destroy him, thus putting an end to this whole war. Unfortunately, I don't know where exactly you will encounter Drelokh since by now he likely may have broken from his rock prison. However, I would assume that once you reach the cliffs, he will have revealed himself along with his army after which he should not be hard to locate. At that point, your largest concern would be reaching him; however, I may again be of some assistance when that time comes.

Now, I believe it is time to not only answer your question pertaining to my knowledge of your quest, but also to lay to rest a simple question that has been following you throughout your quest, quite literally. More than once now on your journey you have crossed paths with a figure hidden within the confines of a cloak, much like the one I wear now. Although they may all appear to be the same you have yet to encounter the same individual twice. Each of these creatures that you have met along your quest all belong to a secret society known as the Guardians Guild. This guild was created to allow wizards of all species to join together and do whatever was necessary in protecting this world, both the lands above and below. To put to rest your inevitable question, no, we can do nothing to stop Drelokh on our own. There are many reasons for this that I may explain to you later if a reason arises. Finally, the reason that each time a guardian has confronted you and his appearance had been hidden is to dispel the fear that would unavoidably follow if he were to reveal himself. As I said, we guardians come from every race and the sight of some would undoubtedly cause an immediate, and irrational panic. There is something that Erquein told you that may be one of the most difficult things for you to judge. There is no race that is purely good, just as there is no race that is purely evil. In the lives of every creature, one question must be decided the truth of the inner conscience. After that question of allegiance has been decided, that creature will continue down that chosen path and the further it travels the harder it is to truly change.

I also am a guardian of this planet, and as such the cloak that protects my body from your eyes has not been removed. Before I revealed myself to you both I wanted to make sure you understood the truth along with the reality of good vs. evil."

After she had finished speaking, Theshius pulled away the cloak that had concealed her body. As she let the cloak fall, invisibly to the ground a loud gasp of shock and surprise escaped the lips of both Tristin and Keeris. What now stood before them was nothing that either of them had expected. Tristin had unconsciously pictured Theshius as a grimp from the first time he heard her name, but even if he had been forewarned would he have not believed this until he saw it.

The beautiful voice that once escaped from behind the cloak suggested a fair and attractive creature, but nothing could be farther from the truth. Standing before Keeris and Tristin was a goblin, a short, stocky, ugly little creature that if it hadn't been for the cloak Tristin and Keeris would have probably run the moment they saw her.

It was at that very instant that Tristin fully realized what Erquein meant when he told him about the goodness coming from an evil race. "I understand, although I wish it didn't take something as potent as this to force me to comprehend it all."

"Well my friends, you have just taken a giant leap in your mission along with the conquest over Drelokh." Theshius had a large smile on her face as she walked over to the bookshelves and started grabbing random books and piled them in her arms when she suddenly paused.

"My word, I hadn't realized how late it had gotten. Please forgive me, we can start your studies tomorrow after you've both have ample rest. If you would follow me, I will show you to your room."

Theshius motioned for them both to follow her as she led them up two more flights of stairs until they reached a sleeping chamber with two beds already made up for her guests. "These beds are extremely comfortable so I would assume you would have no problems resting here. I will see you both in the morning when we shall commence your training. Good night, young ones."

As Theshius began walking back down the steps she stopped and looked back. "Oh, and Keeris you will be joining Tristin in his studies. We have high hopes that you too will become a great wizard."

As Theshius left the room the candles on the walls slowly faded away and the room went dark. Both Keeris and Tristin were too tired to talk so they immediately went to bed. However, Keeris found sleeping rather difficult after learning that he would be doing something that he had not only always dreamed of but also never thought possible, he was going to become a kolerunt sorcerer!

Chapter 15

The Secret Behind the Cloak

It had been a week since Tristin and Keeris had entered the swamps, and two since Tristin had left his village in the east. Every morning, both he and Keeris would wake up and continued to delve deeper into their studies. As each day passed, Tristin and Keeris grew stronger in their skills while every new lesson came easier than the last.

It was a happy and carefree time for both Keeris and Tristin as they learned many deep and dangerous arts that had been hidden for many years. The days passed by with little notice by either of them. All thoughts of their quest and Drelokh seemed to fade as their knowledge along with their newfound abilities, grew. As what had once begun as a simple fire spell had now grown into a flame that could melt metal.

Now, seven months had passed since that dreadful day that Tristin had to watch as his best friend gave up his home in search of peace. A great transition had occurred since then, as both Tristin and Keeris became masters of the magical arts. However, the time had come for them to leave the sanctuary of Theshius' home, to complete the task that had been appointed them.

Tristin and Keeris were just finishing their lunch and as usual, Theshius had left them to eat alone. Tristin and Keeris knew their time with Theshius was running short but there was still so much for them to learn.

"Tristin," Keeris's large eye's never left his plate as he spoke, but his voice was more than enough to reveal his apprehension. "Do, do you suppose that we will be strong enough to defeat Drelokh when the time, time comes?"

"You know Keeris, the more that thought enters my head the better I feel about our chances."

Tristin had a large smile on his face as he spoke with a new confidence. "After I had decided to follow Darius through the forest and before I was able to leave my village, I spoke with a member of the Guardians Guild. Naturally, at the time I had no recollection of the Guild of Guardians or anything good that could be related to this intruder. However, after we got to talking, he told me something that has stuck with me for quite some time and seems to resurface every time I run into some new problem. He told me that no hero could ever fully complete his quest if it weren't for the interference of some friend or ally to help him along the way. Even now, as I think back on all the trials that the forest placed before me, I don't think that I could have made it through ANY of them if it hadn't been for either my determination to find Darius or through the help of a friend I found along the way. So, as long as we stick together, I would say we stand a chance against this great dragon."

That had seemed to been enough to satisfy Keeris and he dropped the subject.

"Well, I see you two have finished with your lunches, wonderful!" Theshius seemed to have developed a knack for walking in on them without their knowing.

"I have something for you both." Theshius

never see the cloak covering your body yet you will know that it is there. The cloak can sense when it needs to protect you from the eyes of the world and when that danger is gone, with it too will vanish your cover. Once you have learned to better control your powers you will also be able to command the will of the cloak to hide your body when you deem it necessary."

Theshius walked over to the side of the room and took her accustomed chair of which she sat while she trained her new companions. Instinctively, both Keeris and Tristin followed Theshius and took their seats next to her. "My young friends, allies, and those newest to the order of the Guardian. Unfortunately, your time here with me has come to an end, for tomorrow you must resume your mission of which you have both been absent far too long. Drelokh has broken the chains of his imprisonment and his army is growing stronger by the day. As I mentioned earlier, the Guardians will be unable to assist you in your plight against the dragon himself. However, you have another ally waiting to join you at the Cliffs of Shemod, I have great hope that with your combined efforts you will be able to put an end to the dragon and his evil ways. No one can teach you how to harness the powers of your cloaks, this is something that you must learn with time and patience. Now there is one last thing we Guardians can do to assist you in your quest, and that we have already done."

Keeris jumped from his seat as if he had just woken from a trance. "Wait a minute, what, what, what do you mean you've already done it. What is it that, that you have done to help?"

Theshius stared deep into Keeris's eyes, yet didn't respond. Theshius simply waited, knowing that the answer would find one of them if she gave it time, and it did.

Tristin's head dropped straight into his hands. "How foolish of me, I don't know how it could have slipped my mind all this time." Keeris began bobbing up and down with interest and excitement. Unfortunately, even Theshius' training was unable to quell the eternal eagerness that Keeris always kept with him, as he was anxious to hear what this last bit of help was. "The last night Keeris and I were in the colivien city I had a lengthy talk with one of the guardians. There were two bits of advice he said that he would leave me with. The first was simply to beware whom I put my trust in, and the second was a book he had given me. However, the book was just a bunch of empty pages so when we arrived, I placed it on the bookshelf and somehow got so caught up with my training here I had completely forgotten about it up until now!"

Tristin jumped from his chair and made a mad dash for the staircase. Keeris, figuring Tristin was making for the book, immediately gave chase. Tristin ran up into his room and quickly dove for the lone book sitting on the shelf near his bed, with Keeris hovering over him with great anticipation.

Theshius had been through this many times since she had trained a great deal of the Guardians herself. With that, she simply waited patiently for both Tristin and Keeris to return with the same confused look that plagued each of her past students when they opened their books.

Without fail, Theshius watched as Keeris and Tristin slowly made their way down the steps with a baffled look in their eyes. Tristin slowly set the book down on the arm of Theshius' chair and sat down with Keeris mimicking his actions.

"The book is still empty! There was no writing, not even on one page, I thought maybe that would have changed now that we are guardians?" Keeris quickly got up and rechecked the book maybe they had just missed the minimal writings in the beginning pages.

"This book given to you by one of the Guardians is one of a select few known as the Colifiate, or more commonly, the Book of Ages. This is a very special book. Nevertheless, you may not fully understand its purpose until your knowledge has greatly increased. This book holds a great magic much likes the cloaks that now secretly cover your bodies. This book will help the two of you in two ways. First, Colifiate will show you things from long ago, these inscriptions of the past will aid you in whatever current dilemma you may find yourself. Secondly, this book can send a message to another Guardian who is in possession of a book himself. This is how I came to know so much about you and your mission without ever setting foot outside my home. Oh, and to answer your question Keeris, yes, you will find a book belonging to you packed away along with your belongings."

Theshius lifted her body from the chair and stretched her arms. "I have some urgent business that I must attend to. I would suggest taking the rest of the day off from any physically straining activities. You will be needing all your strength when you leave tomorrow." Theshius looked both Keeris and Tristin in the eye, smiled, and descended down to one of the lower levels of her home.

"I only wish Darius could see me now. When we were kids we used to pretend we were these great wizards like our town elder Heretius. It's sort of weird to think about how much these past months have changed us." Tristin's head hung low, whenever anything reminded him of his childhood friend it was as if an instant gloom settled over him. "You know Keeris, nothing will ever be the same for us. If either of us ever returns to what we left behind it will be as if we're strangers in some oddly familiar land."

Keeris tilted his head, looked deep into Tristin's eyes and nearly fell out of his chair with laughter. "Would you listen, listen to yourself; you act as if you've just lost, lost everything in your life and have nothing to show for it. Just, just, just think about it for a minute. You've achieved your greatest childhood dream, found, found a new friend, visited a secret colivien city, RODE A DRAGON, and are in the middle, in the middle of an adventure greater than you could have ever dreamed. Now after all of that, you're worrying that you've lost a piece of yourself, mmhhmmm?"

"I know Keeris and you're right. Sometimes it's just hard to leave everything you had behind, even if it is for something greater. How do you manage to always stay optimistic about everything?"

"Well, well, I suppose I just try and put everything into perspective. Regardless of how good things were, they won't be anything more, more than that, a past memory. So, I try, try and look at everything as a new means for living a more eventful life, mmhhmmm."

"Hmm," Tristin got up from his chair and walked over to the bookshelf on the far side of the room. "I wish it was that simple for me to move on, or at least keep things less complicated."

Keeris stood up, walked over to his friend and put a hand on Tristin's shoulder. "Well buddy, I, I don't plan on leaving you to finish this mission on your own so, so, so you can just forget about complicating matters. There, there is one thing that's been bothering me for some time now, mmhhmmm."

Tristin stopped thumbing through the books along the wall and turned around to give Keeris his full attention.

"Theshius told us we, we were to travel to the Cliff of Shemod and meet someone there who, who, who may help us finish this quest, correct? However, I was wondering how, how we were going to get out of these swamps? I don't really think our powers are strong enough to freeze the swamps to walk on top of it, and, and, and up till now we haven't learned any type of spell that would, that would allow us to fly over it, mmhhmmm."

"I know, the same thought has been bothering me ever since Erquein left us here. Still, I think we might be able to rely on Theshius one last time before we leave, since she must have made the trip numerous times." Tristin smiled as he randomly picked a couple of books off of the shelf and returned to his chair, which he fell into letting the cushions enfold his body. "Now, I don't know about you but I'm not going to give this mission of ours any more thought tonight. Theshius told us to relax and that's just what I plan on doing."

Keeris followed Tristin's example and the two of them spent the rest of their last day at the home of Theshius in peace. The two never saw Theshius for the rest of the afternoon and she never showed up to bring Keeris or Tristin their accustomed supper.

The rest of the evening passed slowly as Keeris and Tristin read through the books off the library wall. Not one word had been spoken since their discussion after lunch until late into the night when a mutual decision had been made to get some sleep to further rest their bodies for the trials they would have to face tomorrow.

Chapter 16

Farewell in the Swamps

Keeris awoke just as the rays of the sun peeked over the horizon and began filling the room with sunlight. If it hadn't been for the fact that both Keeris and Tristin would have to say goodbye to Theshius and once again resume their hazardous quest, it would have been a beautiful day in the swamps.

Keeris slowly sat up from his bed while rubbing the sleep from his eyes and stretching his arms high into the air. "Tristin, are you awake?"

"Yeah, I have been for a while now. I've been thinking about our quest and trying to determine the fastest and potentially safest route that we can take."

"Well, well, did you find anything?"

"No," Tristin let out a long yawn as he got out of his bed. "I think we're going to just have to trust in luck, or at least hope for the best."

Tristin and Keeris quickly changed and then began packing their bags when Theshius climbed the stairs and entered their room. Theshius kept a smile on her face but her eyes gave away the hurt that she was feeling. It wasn't often that Theshius had visitors since not many knew of her home hidden within the swamps; so, her main contact with the outside world had been through Colifiate, her Book of Ages.

"Well my new comrades, I suppose the time has come for you to resume your mission. However, I would like to show you one last thing before you leave, something that will greatly assist your march through my swamps and to the Cliffs of Shemod. Now, come with me and I will show you the true secret behind the location of my home."

Keeris and Tristin quickly gathered their things together and followed Theshius down the many flights of stairs until they reached the lower level containing the door to the swamps. Tristin and Keeris exchanged smiles as they were greatly relieved to hear that Theshius would indeed be assisting them in their escape from the swamps.

Theshius had a twinkle in her eye, it was the same glow she seemed to have before she would teach Tristin and Keeris new and wonderful magic. "I believe you are both already aware of the legends pertaining to the portals leading to Broudiun, The Dark Realm. Now Tristin, I understand that you know the location of one of these hidden portals? The portal of Windover, which was accidentally discovered by your lost companion, is one of the seven gates leading to the Dark Realm. The spot where young Keeris stands just so happens to be another of these portals known as the Swamp Gate. Now you may better understand why I would reside in such an awful place. Each of the seven gates are protected by one of the eldest Guardians who will hide the gate from the eyes of the unwary traveler and similarly reveal it to those who may be in need of it. Your friend Darius had to confront the Guardian of Windover before he was granted access to its secret."

"Wait!" Tristin's eyes were burning in a sudden rage. "You mean it was a Guardian that banished Darius to the fate of the Dark Realm? Why?"

Theshius raised a hand to stop Tristin from speaking, since until he stopped no one would be able to squeeze a word in. "You must control your anger Tristin, it is a dangerous thing to judge the decisions of others, especially when you are unaware of each and every aspect of that equation. The decision to send Darius through the Windover gate was based on two very convincing factors. First of all, the speed that Darius could have gained would have been a powerful asset to his quest. Secondly, and by far most importantly, your friend was planning on passing through Deaths Doorway along with the Caves of Arem, which is the dwelling for the foulest of creatures in Trubanius. This path is arguably even more treacherous than the Tunnels of Bhulek that join our world and the Dark Realm. Of all the powers you will gain as you grow in your magical aptitude, none will give you the ability to see things that have yet to happen. So, as a Guardian and defender of this planet, you must remember each of your actions will come at some price, as there are no guarantees and there is very rarely ever one clear answer."

Theshius walked over beside Keeris and gently moved him aside. She then knelt down and pulled back a large rug to reveal a secret door in the floorboards. "Now that you know part of the dangers that lurk under this door, you are both left with numerous options. If you so choose, you may follow these tunnels all the way to the Imp Puddle which lies at the base of the Shemod Cliffs, try your luck with the swamps on foot or whatever other alternatives that you might think up. However, my fellow Guardians, here there is but one truth. This world and its inhabitance are on the verge of war and are in desperate need of your help. Now whether or not you choose to help, or even how you choose to help, is purely up to you. Think it over, I have made you both breakfast and you may state your decision after that."

Theshius pointed out the meal sitting on a table, which she had prepared for them, then left the room.

Tristin and Keeris sat down next to the table and began eating. They were both slightly perplexed after what Theshius had just told them.

"Hey, Keeris, what do you suppose Theshius meant by all that? I mean we decided we were going to see this thing through to the end and I would have thought that when we accepted the cloaks that she would instill a little more faith in us?"

"Maybe she's just, just trying to give us one last, one last chance to get out of this whole mess while there's still a chance, mmhhmmm."

"Either way, I say we follow this tunnel under

the floor and get to the cliffs as soon as possible, how about you?"

Keeris looked up at Tristin with a large smile on his face while slowly reaching his hand out over the floor. The trap door slowly sprung to life and for the first time in over fifty years, it began to open. A loud creaking noise filled the house as the old and brittle hinges began grinding against the aged rust-covered metal. Keeris then lowered his hand and the door fell and hit the floor with a loud thud, leaving the dark hole beneath the home uncovered. The potent smell of must and mold rushed out from the caves and filled the house with an awful stench.

"Wow! If, if, if I had known it was going to smell like that down there, I may have suggested trying our luck in the swamps, or or at least waited for Theshius to return before opening it, mmhhmmm."

Less than a minute had passed before Theshius had realized that the tunnel door had been opened and she immediately returned to the first floor of her house. "So, does this mean you've decided to resume your adventures by way of my tunnel?"

Theshius had a large smile on her face, as she was ecstatic to see how quickly the two decided on which path to take. Before Either Tristin or Keeris could answer her question, she continued. "Well come along then, I believe you have a world to save!"

Keeris knew that he and Tristin had to leave, but there was something that was holding him back. Before Keeris met Tristin, his life was fairly uninteresting as his everyday life held no special memories. However, now Keeris felt he had meaning to his life along with a lifetime of memories packed into a short 7-month period. "Thank, thank you so much for everything Theshius, we will never forget you!" Keeris let a tear fall from his large watery eyes.

"Oh, come now." Theshius walked over to the table and retrieved the packs for her new friends. "You speak as if you're walking to your doom. We will see one another again; I promise you that. Now you must hurry along, you have much ground to cover in a short period of time. So long my friends, may the hardships of your journey quickly become the memories of your footprints. Don't forget, if you need to reach me, I'm always simply a quill away."

Tristin looked at both Keeris and Theshius, took a deep breath to hold back his tears of goodbye, and descended into the darkness of the tunnel. Keeris also followed, but not before running back to give Theshius a hug goodbye, and once again the two young heroes embarked on their quest.

As they reached the bottom of the steps that led to the tunnel floor Tristin bent down and picked up an old rotted bone, and with a wave of his hand the bone began to glow, illuminating the underground corridor.

The two companions walked for hours without saying a word. Neither of them knew exactly which direction they were going but simply hoped that the tunnel would lead them to the Cliffs of Shemod. The underground corridors were exceptionally damp and a strong stench of creatures long decayed filled the air. Strange and eerie sounds occasionally echoed through the stone halls making the young wizards quite nervous as they constantly checked over their shoulders.

Keeris and Tristin were now traveling through a domain that separated and connected the Lands Above with the Dark Realm. These tunnels, known as the Tunnels of Bhulek, were the same passageways by which Darius met an unfortunate end. With that knowledge, Tristin was very uneasy about traveling through them.

Since the two were underground and couldn't use the sun as their clock, neither of them was quite sure what time of day it was. However, many hours had passed since they left the home of Theshius and a numbing sensation in their stomachs told them it was now well past lunchtime. The past months they had spent at the home of Theshius made them both soft to traveling. Theshius had prepared for them some of the finest food either of them had ever eaten, and after all that time it was hard to go back to the rations they had previously become accustomed to.

Not much was said as the two ate their lunch, however it was obvious that a similar feeling was being shared between them, fear. Ever since they had descended down into the tunnels a strange sensation kept overcoming them, the sensation that they were being followed.

Back at the grimp village a great transition had begun to take place. After that dreadful day that Heretius had announced his decision to leave the village, a newfound sense of responsibility engulfed the grimps. Heretius's last command before leaving was that the grimps unite themselves with the other creatures of the forest and prepare for a great battle, and that is exactly what the grimps began to do.

Immediately after Heretius' departure, the grimps banded together to create a task list, a group of duties that had to be carried out. Directly afterward these responsibilities were assigned and a new order began under the banner of a now formulated civilization.

It had been nearly a month that had resided since the shock of Darius and Tristin's departure from the village. At this time, a new period had begun for the grimps as many species, of which were seldom seen in the grimp village, were now coming and going on a daily basis. The small blacksmith that had previously made only pots, pans, and eating utensils for the grimps was now the production grounds for a mass display of weapons. With the combined efforts of the wood elves and the dwarves of Rewick (an eastern mountain range), new techniques were learned for forging the strongest and mightiest of weaponries.

Also abiding by the last wishes of Heretius, the grimps had formed strong alliances with the many surrounding species. The resistance force created by the grimps was now a collection of thirty separate groups of creatures, and was now developing into a formidable army. None of the creatures joined by the alliance knew the true horrors that were assembling in the pits below them. However, one thing was for certain, there was a real and definite need for the joining of their strengths, and they all knew deep down that there was a great change taking place.

All those old enough immediately began training, although they prayed for the best they also prepared for the worst. Along with the newfound alliances, a small band of leaders was assembled. This newly formed group set out to seek the aid of those to the west of the great river, in hopes of further increasing their numbers. Since Tristin and Darius had left, the horror of the forest and the unknown to the west had slowly slipped further and further to the back of the grimps minds. When these two young grimps put aside their fears and left the village, it was as though an imaginary barrier had been destroyed, and with it the terror of the unknown as the whole village now began venturing deeper and deeper into the world to seek new help.

Always, the constant murmur of the names of Darius and Tristin filled the air and was ever present in the back of every grimps mind; those who were brave enough to face the most terrible of fears, to not only be the first to venture out into a world unfamiliar to them but also to do this alone. That thought filled the minds and hearts of every grimp and pushed them to fight harder for their new cause, simply to live without the fear of evil.

Chapter 17

A Friend on the Cliffs

The days passed slowly in the Tunnels of Bhulek. Without the light of the sun to guide them and inform them as to the time, Tristin and Keeris were walking in the endless gloom of night. It was no wonder the creatures of this dark realm were of an evil sort, after only a couple of days in the damp and darkness of the caves, Tristin and Keeris were not only beginning to lose all hope but with it their sanity.

The feeling that they were being followed never left the two travelers. Constant sounds of footsteps and muffled voices filled their heads as the shadows, cast by Tristin's light, haunted their progression. Their eyes were continually darting to each flicker of light and every outcrop within the tunnel, always waiting to be met by the voiceless creature they all too often thought they heard stalking them through the tunnels. The fact that neither Keeris nor Tristin knew where they were, or even which direction they were headed, added to their misery. Without the hope brought about by the changing of their surroundings and the passing of each day, which they were able to witness for themselves when they traveled through the forest, their burden grew heavier along with their hearts.

It was the beginning of what Tristin and Keeris thought to be their fourth day since entering these forsaken underground passages. With the exception of the constant fears that they were being followed, nothing ever changed within the tunnels. Never did either of the wizards encounter any monsters lurking about in the caverns, with exception of the long-deceased remains of many different-sized creatures, and neither did their surroundings seem to change much. Although the tunnels curved and turned quite frequently, it never seemed to change in its appearance or size. The horrible stench that had once poured into the home of Theshius, when the trap door was first opened, was now no more than a forgotten nuisance as they eventually became accustomed to the pungent odor.

The day was again growing long and both Tristin and Keeris were on the verge of insanity. The lack of natural light along with the openness of the forest had become a long-lost memory that now seemed more like a distant dream that they both longed for. The muffled echoes of the tunnel had finally pushed Tristin over the edge, he needed to hear or see something other than the same simple rock walls. Tristin took a deep breath and opened his mouth to let out as loud a scream as his lungs could handle when something stopped him. The artificial light that had guided them all this way suddenly changed from a light glowing blue to a radiant green, then to a bright red, and then to a yellow. The light appeared as if it were escaping from the bone in Tristin's hand and was going straight through the wall.

Tristin and Keeris quickly exchanged curious glances and slowly followed the light right up to the side of the rock wall. The light appeared to pass through the rock as if there was nothing there. Reluctantly, Keeris reached out to touch the rock face and his hand followed the light straight through the wall!

"This, this, this wall is only an illusion!" Within a matter of seconds, Keeris' attitude turned from that of near madness to a familiar happiness that he had felt when he first saw the colivien city.

Tristin and Keeris longed to have the horrible solitude of the tunnel behind them and without hesitation passed through the illusion. Behind the wall was a flight of stone stairs cut into the rock with the same haphazard manner that the tunnel followed. So, with the hope of again seeing the light of the sun and their spirits renewed, they followed the stairs as fast as their legs could carry them. The ascent was much longer than that which they followed from Theshius's home to the tunnels. The two seemed to climb for hours with no end in sight as the muscles in their legs burned from this new exercise. Their breaths were coming in short and heavy bursts as they slowed their pace, forcing their bodies to move on when they finally saw it. Squinting their eyes through the sweat rolling down their foreheads, they approached a large stone door that appeared to be carved directly into the side of the rock wall.

The stone weighed more than either of them could have ever managed on their own, at least before their journey began. Fortunately, they were now Guardians and well versed in the magical arts. So, with the wave of Keeris' hand the door slowly ground open and the two slipped through.

Their demeanor dropped as they passed

through the door as they longed for the natural light of the sun and the fresh air of the worlds above. However, the light they saw was not that of the sun. There were many candles affixed to the wall that illuminated a large, round, stone room. Against one wall was a fireplace that was still smoldering from a fire that had been just recently extinguished. Along the rest of the wall was a long bookshelf that wrapped the rest of the way around the room with the exception of the fireplace along with a small desk that parted the two sides of the shelf. The floor was covered with a large and beautifully woven rug containing a pattern that looked somewhat like the shadow of a dragon. Finally, in the center of the room was a familiar round wooden table surrounded with chairs, one of which contained a large, black cloaked figure that was staring directly at them.

Tristin was about to blurt out an apology for the intrusion when he noticed out of the corner of his eye that a similar black cloak also hid Keeris. Tristin then quickly examined himself to discover that he too was clad in the dressings of a Guardian.

There was a long silence as both Keeris and Tristin stood next to a door that hadn't been opened for nearly fifty years. Nevertheless, the Guardian who sat at the table was expecting these visitors and with the nod of his head, two chairs moved away from the table signifying Keeris and Tristin to sit.

"So, I presume you are Keeris and Tristin, the newest two to the order of the Guardians. My name is Gregor, and I am the guardian of the mountain passage."

"Then we've reached the Cliffs of Shemod!" The thought of not having to descend back into those awful tunnels was great news and Tristin nearly lit up with excitement.

"Well, you haven't technically reached the cliffs yet, my friends. My home lies on the foothills just west of the mountains themselves. Come, let me show you." Gregor rose from his chair and led both Tristin and Keeris outside his home.

As the three Guardians stepped foot outside the home of Gregor, the door slammed solidly behind them. The sound of the door slamming shut echoed through the foothills and Tristin and Keeris impulsively turned around to locate the source of the noise. It was simple magic but still left the two new wizards in awe. Gregor's home was built directly into an enormous boulder and the door from which they had just emerged was now completely hidden, not even the crack of a doorsill was still present.

Tristin and Keeris began to search the side of the rock for any breaks that might indicate where a door once resided, but it was perfectly smooth. "You must have learned by now that each gate is not only guarded by an elder Guardian but also by magic. The gate that lies beneath this rock is cloaked with a spell so that even magic folk like yourselves would struggle to locate it. The lands of Broudin and the connecting tunnels are not a place anyone should ever travel lightly. However, that isn't the purpose of which I brought you both out here, not for the moment anyway. This mountain range that you see before you is not in truth the Cliffs of Shemod, this range is known as the Wall of Bouwind. On the other side of Bouwind lies the Calembour Valley, which separates the Wall of Bouwind from the Cliffs of Shemod. From what I understand your current path is within the Cliffs of Shemod themselves. Nevertheless, if you so choose, you will not have to complete the remainder of your journey alone." Gregor then pointed high upon an outcropping in the cliffs, "There is the one who wishes to join your cause."

Although the sun was now very low in the sky its light was still enough to reveal the silhouette of a black figure standing at the edge of a high up cliff. This creature too was dressed in the fabric of a Guardian and looked as if he were a stone gargoyle gazing upon the farthest reaches of Trubanius searching for some hidden truth.

Gregor turned around and tapped the side of the large boulder and the concealed doorway was once again exposed. "Well my friends, it is getting late in the afternoon and these mountains aren't safe to travel by night. You are both more than welcome to stay, and in the morning, you can meet your new companion."

Tristin and Keeris hesitantly followed Gregor into his home as they were both extremely curious about the identity of this new guardian. Also, it had been so long since they had breathed in the fresh outdoor air that retreating back into the rocks wasn't a pleasant thought. Gregor invited his two guests to sit at the table while he began preparing some food for his guests to eat before they were to head off to bed. Tristin and Keeris were filled with questions and wanted to know everything they could about the mountain, the Calembour Valley, and this Guardian who wished to join them. Knowingly, Gregor placed a bowl of thick and creamy soup in front of them as he also sat and began to tell them what he could, and what might be useful for them to know.

"I was expecting you to have many questions about the remainder of your journey, however it's much too late in the afternoon to tell you all you will need to know so I will try and tell you that which will be most important for you. First of all, we have

Calembour Valley, which is well deserving of its name.
The valley is unlike any other you will ever encounter,
since it is essentially alive. The valley is said to have
a split personality, it can be the most beautiful place
you have ever seen with lush green grass, crystal
clear ponds, a cloudless sky, and trees with the most
succulent fruit you have ever tasted. However, in the
next minute the valley can change into an awful place
that can bring your worst nightmares to reality and
for this reason, has caused the death of thousands of
unwary travelers. There are those that believe the
Valley is like a mirror that reflects the deepest
feelings of its travelers. So, when you are at peace
with yourself and happy at heart so is the valley;
conversely, if there is any hate or anger that dwells
within you, the valley will grow cold and become that
anger. Once you have reached the western side of
the Calembour Valley you must cross the River Onyx.
The river is as uncertain and ever changing as the
valley, as there are two sources to this river. First,
there is the flawlessly pure water that flows from
the highest tip of Shemod. When these waters reach
the valley floor they are joined by a natural spring,
which emits the blackest of waters from the pits of
the Dark Realm, making these waters dangerous and
unpredictable. If it weren't for the necessity of your
haste, I would advise you to add two days to your
journey and go around the river and the Imp Puddle,
which it empties into. After crossing the River Onyx,

you will reach the Cliffs of Shemod along with the true means of your quest. It is here that you must now confront Drelokh and destroy him."

Gregor paused as he noticed that the Tunnels of Bhulek had taken its toll on Tristin and Keeris, who were both using their arms to keep their heads propped up. "My friends, follow me, I will show you to your sleeping chambers. We may yet have some time to discuss your journey in the morning before you take your leave."

Gregor guided his two weary guests through a small door and into a bedroom, which like the other rooms of the house was built directly into the stone. It didn't take long before both Keeris and Tristin were fast asleep and dreaming of their adventures to come.

The night passed by quickly and uneventfully as the morning sun rose, bringing the start of a new day filled with adventures for Tristin and Keeris. Gregor had already been awake since the first hints of light ascended over the horizon and had been waiting for his guests to wake up.

Tristin and Keeris slowly pulled their bodies out of bed and walked into the main room of the home, which also contained the door leading back down to the Tunnels of Bhulek. As they entered the room, they were struck by a strong aroma coming from a pot over the fireplace as Gregor immediately acknowledged them.

"Ah, I see you two have finally awoken! Here, have yourselves a seat while I get you something for breakfast." Gregor quickly found two bowls, which he filled with the gruel he had been cooking over the fire. "Here, eat this. It may not taste the greatest, but it will give you the strength you need to climb over the Wall of Bouwind."

Gregor was right, the food that he served Tristin and Keeris was horrible and took some effort for them to swallow. However, they could feel the warmth of the food spread throughout their bodies. After polishing off their bowls and earnestly refusing seconds, Tristin and Keeris grabbed their belongings and headed out the front door with Gregor.

"My friends, before you leave, I want you to take this knowledge with you. These next few days may just as well be the worst you will ever have faced. But, be assured that good can always prevail over evil if you follow your heart and trust in the power that lies within yourself. Also, be wary of Drelokh for he will have learned from his past mistakes and will be expecting any type of misdirection you might throw at him. It is unfortunate that your mission has changed so greatly from the short time ago you left your village. However, we can't change the past and now the state of the world anxiously awaits its new future. Now go, you have a friend who has been tirelessly awaiting your arrival for several days on top of that cliff. I pray that with your combined talents and cunning you will find a way to bring light back into a world being overtaken by darkness."

Gregor watched as the last and only hope the world had for peace climbed the great cliffs straight for Drelokh to a most certain doom. "It seems like only yesterday I had to watch as the young Guardians climbed those great cliffs in hopes of saving all they loved, only then there were five." Gregor bent down and filled his hand with the dirt lying on the ground, letting it slowly fall through his hands as an easterly wind carried it away. "You three carry the hopes of all that is good in the world, make us proud. Good luck my friends, good luck."

There was a well-established path that followed the face of the mountain, leading up towards the cliffs, so the morning hike wasn't overly strenuous for either Tristin or Keeris. It took most of the morning for the two to reach the spot where they were to meet with this new comrade. Tristin and Keeris were both trying to guess who and, more importantly, what this friend of theirs was going to be. Keeris thought that he would be a creature of the underworld like Theshius while Tristin was expecting something more refined like a colivien or an elf. After roughly 30 minutes of climbing the two noticed a familiar feeling as their cloaks suddenly covered their bodies hiding their appearances. Yet this time neither of the two were caught by surprise as they had been when first meeting Gregor.

As the two travelers rounded the next corner a fellow Guardian, whose physical characteristics were completely hidden from their sight, immediately confronted them.

"I have been waiting quite some time to again meet up with you my friend." By the sound of his voice, the creature hidden beneath the magical cloak had suffered through much. "For the last several days I've sat upon this hill, hoping and praying as I watched the two of you battle the Tunnels of Bhulek. It greatly lifts my spirits to see you again and I'm hoping that this time we could endure the hardships of the journey together"

Keeris quickly stepped forward, reaching out to shake hands with the mysterious Guardian. "We would, would both be honored if you would join, join us. It looks like the next couple of days will be really tough, really tough. Only, I have one question, you said you've met one of us before and I was wondering who, who you are, mmhhmmm?"

The Guardians voice became extremely choppy and his breaths seemed to come in short gasps as if he were holding back from crying. "It now all seems so long ago, but I once knew your friend Tristin and he once knew me. I once fell victim to the torments of the Tunnels of Bhulek and tried with every fiber of my being to escape. You see I was once Tristin. I was once the one who was to save this planet. I was the one who you, Tristin, once followed through the forest intending to offer your life for our friendship." The cloaked creature let a tear fall as he dropped the protection of the cloak from around his body.

"No, you can't be..." Tristin's whole body grew white as he fell to his knees, over stricken with emotions. Through clouded, tear-filled eyes Tristin saw the vision of the friend whom he had forced himself to believe was dead. It was Darius!

Chapter 18

Darkness Brews

There was nothing that could be said or done to wipe the smiles off both Tristin's and Darius's faces. It had been over half a year since the two friends had last seen one another, however their adventures and trials had seemed to age them many years further. Even Keeris was excited when he learned it would be Darius who would be joining them. After listening to Tristin talk about him over and over, he felt as if they were old friends as well.

Tristin was in exceptionally high spirits as they continued on, nearly skipping along the mountain path. "So, Darius, I know that you followed the Tunnels of Bhulek by way of the Windover Pond Gate, but what happened to you after that? I mean, even the Guardians said they were unsure as to what really happened to you and thought you must not have made it very far through the tunnels."

It was apparent that the paths Darius had traveled definitely took their toll on him as even now he had a look of fatigue in his eyes as he spoke. "Well, it's actually quite a long story, but for now I will spare you from some of the darker details. I had just faced off against the Guardian of Windover, who at the time I thought was some evil witch bent on destroying me. Well, after a short and somewhat pathetic fight on my part, I was left to live with a short warning about confronting her again. Anyway, the next day I found myself lying on the grass in a beautiful clearing next to the Windover Pond and decided to clean off and take a refreshing swim. Well, that's when I found a passage to the tunnels, which of course I had no recollection of at the time. After following the tunnels for a while, I came across a couple of orcs who were a little more excited to find me than I was to find them. I almost escaped from them but was caught within a few feet from the caves entrance and was kept in a cage for dinner. Luckily for me, I knew Heretius's little flame spell and escaped from the orcs who, unfortunately discovered me in the escape and chased me through the tunnels."

Darius had both Keeris and Tristin hanging on his every word. If not for the simple fact that he was right in front of them telling the story, he would have thought they were concerned he wouldn't make it out alive. "Anyway, while I was trying to escape down the tunnels I ran straight into a stalactite and fell unconscious. As I saw everything go black, I thought I had died and the orcs would finish off what was left of me. However, I seem to be blessed with some unnaturally good luck. When I woke up, I found myself in a little home, which... was more of a furnished cave carved into the side of the tunnel. There were these crazy little creatures that heard me running from the orcs and pulled my body from their reach at the last second, so I owed these little creatures my life. Well, it just so happens that these creatures, who called themselves Qwuints, were not only friendly to our cause but were delighted to help me out! After they healed me and made me some clothes, they showed me a secret passage, which happened to be a couple of days journey in the dark. When I finally reached the exit, I found myself at the home of Oliphius, Guardian of the Cliffside Passage. It was from both him and another guardian that I learned my powers and was then offered the life of a Guardian, which I see you two also accepted. Well, I guess that about sums it up for my trip, I have been in contact with Theshius who told me a little about your travels, but I would like to hear from the both of you what exactly you've been through these past months."

"Wait a minute!" Tristin stopped dead in his tracks and Keeris almost ran directly into him. "If you met a guardian only days after I lost you why didn't Theshius know you were still alive?"

"Well, it turns out Oliphius isn't much for keeping in contact with his fellow guardians. In fact, it wasn't until well after I accepted the cloak that he even remembered to give me my Colifiate."

The rest of the afternoon flew by as Tristin and Keeris told the story of their own adventures as Darius listened with great interest. As the three travelers continued walking along the mountains of Bouwind and shared their stories, they were pleasantly surprised to see that they had nearly reached Calembour Valley and the sun was nearly moments from disappearing behind the horizon. Content with their location, the three travelers decided to set up camp and prepare themselves for an early start to what would hopefully be an equally simple journey through the valley of Calembour.

Not too far away, deep within the impenetrable carcass of the Cliffs of Shemod, a great host of beasts from the underworld had assembled. It was the Chamber of Death, an ancient meeting place for the leaders of the old Black Banner. Now the great torches, which encompassed the room, had once again been relit and an all too familiar face had once more regained his place as their chieftain. A countless number of the Black Banner's leaders gathered tightly around their leader, awaiting his command.

Drelokh slowly lifted his head and began to survey his followers as a luminous flame of vengeance flickered in his eye. He, the great dragon and leader of the Black Banner, had managed to free himself from the bonds of that great rock that held him prisoner all these years. However, his years of imprisonment had caused him to grow weak and he dared not attack the residence of Trubanius until he had regained his power and control over the creatures of the underworld. Now, for the first time in over three hundred years, Drelokh addressed his followers to once again lead them into the heat of battle.

Drelokh's voice was deep and terrible. It sounded as if he growled when he spoke, and as his words reverberated off the cave walls they could be felt as much as heard. "You pathetic, insolent fools! Far too long have you been forced to live in these demeaning and sordid holes beneath the surface.

Regardless of however fitting it may be to the darkness and malice that dwells within you, it must now end! We have all allowed ourselves to be banished to these lowly pits by a race far less superior to our own. Nevertheless, our days of crawling through the darkness are growing few, for soon we shall unveil our forces to the cowards above and drive them into the depths of the planet, to live a life that has plagued us all far too long. Our enemy has begun to ally themselves together! They think that by gathering their forces of pathetic and untaught fighters they might stand some chance against us. FOOLS!" Drelokh lifted his head high into the air and engulfed the rocky ceiling with his fiery breath which caused the rocks to begin to melt. Once his fire had died down, he again reeled back and released an ear-piercing roar, which was fueled by his built-up hate and aggression towards his enemies that banished him to this fate.

"Spread the word and make it known that the time for our revenge is upon us! Leave me now, gather your forces as we have planned! For tomorrow we shall break from our prison and have our vengeance on all those who oppose us! We shall be the beginning of a new age on Trubanius and all its riches will be ours!"

The room immediately filled with cries of

delight as all present raised their weapons of destruction in approval for their leader. Shortly after, all those who had gathered within the Chamber of Death withdrew their forces to prepare for the coming war that was promised them by Drelokh. All, with the exception of two.

Audric, who had been the chief commander alongside Drelokh during the Great War, remained with the red dragon after everyone else had left. There were few who had ever seen Audric's true attributes since he, like the Guardians, kept his body veiled behind a long black cloak.

"Master." Audric seemed to always be aware of his surroundings as his eyes flashed back and forth from beneath his cloak, searching for any prying ears. "My lord, as you well know, I have been keeping an ever-watchful eye on our young adversary."

The red dragon lowered his long scaly neck so he could look straight into Audric's eyes. "Captain, I no longer need you ever-present at my side, I have a new task for you. I want you to take whatever forces you deem necessary and intercept these young Guardians before they reach the eastern cliffs of Shemod and Dragon Rock. Even the most inexperienced of Guardians know to fear the River Onyx, now go and teach these two why."

Audric gracefully fell to one knee and bowed his head before the dragon. "Consider it done my lord, and this time there will be nothing to get in our way." Audric lifted his body back to an upright position and swiftly left Death's Chamber, beginning his own mission to find and destroy the guardians.

At the base of a large mountain in the Shemod mountain range, a billowy cloud of black smoke began to form. This was Dragon Rock, the heart and soul of Drelokh's army. Upon these grounds the army known as the followers of the Black Banner began to assemble. Over three centuries ago the Black Banner would march through the countryside destroying and pillaging everything that had gotten in its way. These were the great dragon's elite, and merely mentioning the name of the Black Banner would instill paralyzing fear in the hearts of any who would oppose them. Now all these years later, a bloodthirsty lust for death and destruction lured a new regime of warriors from Broudiun together to once again reign terror on their enemies.

Slowly, the hazy light of the sun disappeared behind the cliffs of Shemod as the warriors of the Black Banner begin their march from Dragon Rock on some secret mission that would surely bring with it the toils of another great war.

Chapter 19

The Council of Athrox

There are a few simple things in the world that have faultless reliability. One of these is the certainty that the darkness of the night will eventually be shattered by the return of the sun. With that, the three curled up masses, the newest to the guardian order, lie in a deep sleep on the plains of the Calembour Valley. They were slowly wakened by the warm and pleasant touch of the morning sun as it chases away the chills of the autumn night.

Slowly Darius, Tristin and Keeris opened their eyes and began to shake off the remains of a satisfying and unusually restful night's sleep. The joy that came hand-in-hand with the reuniting of lifelong friends held fast as the three quickly ate their breakfast and made ready to begin the second day of a unified journey; completely unaware of the terrible dangers that began their flight down the mountain cliffs in pursuit of them during the night.

Tristin had a slight hop to his stride as he surveyed the valley, keeping a vigilant eye out for anything that might seem out of the ordinary. "So, tell me, why was it that we were to be so cautious about entering this valley? It seems like a rather peaceful place if you ask me."

Darius had been preoccupied watching Keeris happily skipping along in front of them so it took some time for the question to catch up with him. "What? Oh. Well, I'm not entirely certain what the reasoning was behind the warning. However, I would think it would be wise to follow the advice given to us by one of the guardians."

"Well, I suppose your right." Tristin was instantly drawn back to the memories of his trials in the forest before meeting Keeris, along with the thoughts of the things that were soon to come. "It's all just so hard to believe. I mean, how could all of this have happened? Why now, and why us? Don't you ever wonder just what would have happened if you had said, No! Or, if I could have only caught up with you before you entered Windover Pond?"

Darius had a somewhat timeworn look about him as he turned to Tristin with a half-drawn smile on his face. "My friend... I believe I have learned more about myself and this world in the past seven months than I might have ever learned if a lifetime had I stayed back at our village. As a result of everything that has happened, I've learned a few very important lessons in life. One of the most important of these being never to question a past judgment!" The smile on Darius's face grew as he paused and thought back on the choices he had made over the past few months. There was a sense of accomplishment in his smile as he patted Tristin on the back, urging him to continue the pace. "It's one of the worst feelings in the world, self-criticism. However impossible it may be to block out completely, forcing myself to think positively has played a vital role in helping me through the darker portions of this past year. It's in that logic that I believe your question of, what if, might justly be the worst one you could ask. Since there's nothing you can do about your past decisions, dwelling on them and forgetting to live in the present would be unfair to the choices you did make. As I said, that question had haunted me ever since I left the protection of the village that day. But, if it hadn't been for that decision, I would have never gained the experiences, wisdom, or the friendship that I have now. And likewise, you would have never met Keeris here. We are together again, and for now nothing else matters. Like a great friend of mine once told me, when we return from this journey we will be known as the heroes of the world. No one will live and not know the names of Tristin, Keeris or Darius and they will write books about us and tell the tales of our adventures for the rest of time! Now that, my friend, is a powerful consequence of a, what if."

Keeris simply shook his head and laughed at the topic being discussed by his friends as he continued to skip along. "Well, well, well my philosopher friends, step lively, we should be reaching the River Onyx before supper time, mmhhmmm."

The faintest whisper echoed throughout the lands of Trubanius. The rumor of war once again threatened the lands and its inhabitance as a long-lived time of peace was coming to an untimely end. There was a massive gathering of creatures in a large clearing, hidden somewhere in the vast forests of Trubanius. It was here that a great alliance had been forged as the call of evil and the promise of destruction had refueled an ancient bond between many of the creatures that lived on the surface. Amongst this clearing, a circle of enormous rocks had been erected. This circle had been a bond, a circle of trust and friendship between those opposing the great dragon. It was now time to rebuild that amity.

Over fifteen hundred years ago, long before the Great War, and long before the red dragon's claim to evil. Long before the splitting of the world into the lands above and below. It was the Age of Unification, a time when all the creatures of the world lived together; although not completely in harmony, it was enough to tolerate one another. It was in this age that Athrox was constructed. Athrox was then to be known as the gathering place for the leaders of every race and also a place where no battles, bloodshed or warfare of any type was to be tolerated. This place was a safe haven for all those needing shelter and protection. Although the true meaning and purpose behind Athrox's construction was lost during the passing of time and the changing of ages, it still held an important role in the development of every age.

Long ago a great alliance had been assembled here with a single purpose, to save the world and end the tyranny of Drelokh. It was for this very reason a council had once again gathered. Creatures from every race had gathered around the massive stone structure of Athrox, awaiting the direction and guidance of their leaders.

Within the center of the stone ring a large elevated platform had been constructed. This platform's main purpose was to help create an environment where a speaker could easily be heard and seen by a massive crowd. It was on top of this center stone platform that seven chairs had been erected, of which six currently held figures donning black robes.

It was late in the morning before a word was spoken by any of the six cloaked beings. Yet finally, as all those who had been summoned to Athrox had arrived, the meeting could now begin.

Slowly and with great poise, one of the six rose from his chair and began to address the crowd. "Friends, companions, and all those who stand upon the plains of Trubanius and call it home. You are all aware of the situation that has arisen over these past few months and along with it the purpose behind the calling of this meeting. Therefore, I would like to hurry this conference along so that we may make better use of the precious hours of peace we still have. I have received word that the armies of the Black Banner have left their stronghold. They are now advancing on the premise that they will be able to destroy us before we can formulate a proper plan of defense. They also have a secondary motive, and that is to swiftly destroy our greatest chance for success. There are currently 3 of our own, deep within the confines of our enemy's territory. Even they don't fully understand the importance of their mission, yet our survival rests so strongly on their success. Similarly, many years ago, back when the red dragon began his reign of tyranny there were five young protagonists. Although those five young heroes didn't seem special to anyone at the time, there was a reason they were selected among Trubanius to be its victors. They were the five that entrapped the dragon and helped bring about this last 300 years of peace. There are now three young warriors, chosen in the same manner by the guardians of our world, to again protect us. They have sacrificed everything for this sole mission and it is by that love and goodness in their hearts that I have rested my faith in them. Still, the powers they wield are not enough to save this world alone! Its own, every creature big and small, every inhabitant of Trubanius, must rise up and fight alongside them!"

With his voice reverberating off the stone pillars of Athrox, the cloaked figure raised his staff into the sky. In a burst of blue flames, the staff ignited as the guardian swirled it around his head. "FRIENDS! We will not let those chosen few fight our battle for us. We will write our own history and preserve our lands for our future generations. Let us bring the fight back to the red dragon and show him once and for all where his stake on our soil lands. The army of the Black Banner advances on us! Join me as we purge their evil from our lands! FOR

TRUBANIUS AND THE LANDS ABOVE!"

Chapter 20

The Storm

The Calembour Valley offered very little cover to anyone caught walking in its wide-open fields. From high above, the valley had the appearance of a large bowl. The walls of the Shemod mountain range fully encompassed the valley with its sharp and jagged cliffs. The only safe passage through the valley was a single dirt path that cut through the valley from the east cliffs, over the Onxy river, and into the cliffs to the west. The sheer mountain face made access to or from the valley nearly impossible by any other means. That is unless anyone were foolish enough to travel through the black waters of the river which cut south through the mountains.

The three young wizards, Darius, Tristin and

The Storm

Keeris had walked the entire day through the valley. In what had started out as a carefree morning was now weighing on the three. Even though they could clearly see the black river as soon as they descended into the valley it felt as though they would never reach it. One of the many natural illusions of the valley was that since it was so flat and there were no trees or large landmarks, distance was extremely difficult to judge. Therefore, after a full day's travel on what the three thought would have been a few hour hike only positioned them about halfway through the valley.

Tristin kicked his foot through a thick, soft plot of grass that was found grown sporadically throughout the vast plain. "Not that I'm looking forward to finally meeting up with this dragon but why does it feel we've been walking for hours and not getting any closer to that stupid river! There aren't even any trees here for us to make a campfire from and not to mention any shelter if the weather turns on us!"

"Oh my, oh my goodness did you see that?" Keeris quickly grabbed Darius by the sleeve and pointed at one of the tuffs of grass Tristin had kicked. Where a soft green plot of grass once rested was suddenly swallowed up and replaced with a barren plot of dirt. The two stopped in their tracks, eyes wide as they watched Tristin plod onward complaining about the valley. With each step Tristin took the ground beneath his feet seemed to melt away leaving nothing but dry soil in his wake. Then slowly the same reaction seemed to be taking place in an arc around him, spreading further and further into the valley erasing the beautiful green grass with a lifeless soil.

"Tristin! Tristin you have to stop!" Darius cried out but Tristin seemed unable to hear his friend's plea. Without waiting another moment Darius rushed Tristin, sprang high into the air and tackled him before he could take another step.

"Darius, what in the world are you doing! That hurt, you could have at least tackled me in the soft grass instead of…" Tristin's eyes grew doubled in size as he scanned his surroundings. The arc of dirt still continued to grow from where the two laid on the ground. "What is happening? Darius, what is this place!?"

"The valley is alive!" Keeris walked over and helped both his friends up off the ground. "Don't you remember what, what Gregor said? The valley is like a mirror and reflects the feelings of its travelers, mmhhmmm!"

"Keeris is right", Darius helped wipe the dirt from his friend's clothes. "This place follows our emotions so we can't give it anything to feed off of! From now on, we must force ourselves to think only happy thoughts."

Tristin closed his eyes tightly and forced his body to relax, trying with all his conscious might to think of only pleasant things. The dirt circle around the three had reached out nearly 100 feet in every direction before the spreading stopped. Anxiously the three watched and waited, was the dirt circle done growing? Would the green grass again sprout now that their thoughts were cheerful once again? After five minutes of waiting nothing changed, the dirt neither grew nor subsided so the three decided they had better continue on.

As they made their way to the edge of the dirt ring Tristin tentatively placed his foot on the soft green grass wondering if the grass would remain. With a sigh of relief, nothing further seemed to happen and again the travelers continued on.

"That was really crazy, guys!" Tristin had rediscovered the joy he had when they first entered the valley. "This place really isn't all that bad if you understand it. I can't believe Gregor said it was so dangerous."

It was now late in the afternoon but the light of the moon through a cloudless sky allowed them to

unison. "What! Let us sleep just a bit longer."

At that point, Keeris was already on top of them pushing them to get up. "Guys your cloaks! You're wearing your cloaks!"

Their eyes snapped open as both Darius and Tristin followed suit with Keeris. First in shock and then immediately searching the horizon.

"It's over there, across the river." Keeris pointed far off in the distance to a steady stream of smoke rising from what looked like a camp at the base of the Shemod mountains on the eastern pass. "What, what, what should we do?"

The now fully cloaked wizards stared at each other looking for advice they knew wouldn't be found. If they turned and retreated, they would lose a full day just getting to the western pass and then days further trying to navigate the mountains. Or they could advance on the river and whatever was camped beyond with no means of hiding or evading a possible enemy.

As the three planned their next move a strong swift breeze pushed them all a step backwards. It was then that they noticed the black clouds moving swiftly into the valley. Within minutes the once beautiful cloudless sky was now a torrent ocean, with clouds battling each other as they churned around one another.

"We need to make for the eastern pass!" Darius grabbed their bags and tossed Tristin and Keeris theirs. "If we get caught up in this storm too long we will never make it all the way back, we need to push on and make it to the river! Iluco eviced, etidnocsba son a eicaf aus." Without hesitating while he ran towards the river, Darius quickly cast a spell on himself and his companions. "That spell has come in handy while living in the mountain these last few months. It's not foolproof but will help deceive the weak-minded eyes from seeing us! I just hope between the spell and the rain that we will be able to slip past whoever or whatever is waiting for us up ahead."

The sky continued to darken as the clouds continued to angrily swirl around one another. Then, without warning, the clouds opened and unleashed a cascade of rain that poured down in a frenzy. Within seconds Darius, Tristin and Keeris were soaked down to the bone. The howling winds tore through their water-laden cloaks and the freezing rain felt like teeth biting into their skin. Pools of water began to form as the ground couldn't absorb the water as fast as the rains fell. If they hadn't just awoken to the morning sunlight they would have sworn that it was still the middle of the night. Squinting their eyes through the harsh rains the sky was nearly black. Somewhere up ahead was the Onyx River but they couldn't make out the ground they were running on nevertheless see a massive river still a mile ahead of them.

"We can't lose the path!" Darius screamed into the wind, unsure if his friends, only feet away, could even hear him over the tempest. He had studied the mountains for a week while waiting for his friend to show up from the underground path and knew the dangers it presented. "We need to cross at the bridge! Keep to the path, we can't swim that river!"

"What path? I can't even see my feet!" Tristin nearly fell as a huge gust of wind slid him backwards on the slick muddy surface of the valley floor.

In an instant the skies cried out, the sound of a massive explosion echoed across the valley as a blinding flash of light shot from the sky. The bolt of lightning hit the northern wall of the valley sending boulders flying from the face of the mountain. In the same instant, the powerful arc of light lit up the sky, for a brief moment the world went from nearly black to as bright as day. It was within that moment the three saw what lay ahead. Within a few hundred yards was the now torrential rivers of the Onyx. The water was rushing so fast and hard that white caps had formed as the waves crashed over the stone banks. Then on the far side of the river, they could see the encampments. A massive army must have set their camp as the storm clouds began to roll in. The entire eastern bank was covered in tents, the wizards had found the army of the red dragon!

"Stay fast, we need to run past those tents! If this rain keeps up and my spell holds, we should be able to slip past them! If we get separated for any reason we will regroup at the top of the mountain on the eastern pass!" Darius slipped in the mud as he looked back to yell to his friends. Quickly, with Keeris's help, he pulled his body from the filth and continued on in the direction of the bridge.

"What happens if…" Keeris's voice was lost as another blast of lightning launched itself from the clouds and exploded on a tent near the northern waters edge. As the blinding light again illuminated the valley the three wizards could see, they were nearly to the bridge which had two large battle-ready orcs standing guard. As soon as the light again faded in the sky it was replaced by the blast of thunder as it echoed throughout the valley shaking the ground and pounding through their chests.

There was no turning back, they had finally reached the Onyx bridge. The waters had broken over the bank of the river and the three had to wade through waist-deep water to reach the base of the bridge. The three were nearly frozen with fear, their intense shaking along with a lump in their throat made it difficult to breathe. This was the true test. They had the powers and abilities to take down the two guards standing watch on the bridge through the storm, but if they did anything to alert the others, they would have no chance in fighting off an entire army! Crouching low, they could only hope and pray that Darius' spell kept them hidden as they slouched past.

"Captain Boskik is a jerk! Why do we always get stuck with the grunt duty?" The orcs hardly seemed to mind the rains pelting against their faces and they carried on a conversation as if the storm wasn't even there. "Just because the dragon selected him as a captain, he thinks he so high and mighty, he isn't even part of the black banner."

Darius and Keeris quickly darted between the orcs and ran off into the camp. The spell had done its trick and the guards hadn't noticed them. Tristin on the other hand wasn't ready to leave just yet, he had a feeling these orcs weren't done so he decided to wait just a bit longer.

"We should have been in the red banner!" One of the orcs continued to complain to his comrade who seemed to be off in his own world. "It's not fair that they get to raid south while we're stuck here. They get a whole village to destroy while we have to sit here and wait for a couple of puny wizards."

Tristin was satisfied with the information he'd heard, now he knew there were at least two armies they needed to face. Quickly he started across the bridge to catch up with Keeris and Darius when something horrible happened. As soon as he passed between the guards he could feel the spell Darius had cast on him wore off. Without hesitation, Tristin threw his body off the side of the stone bridge into the river.

"Did you see that? I saw a big rabbit jump in the water!" The guard who had been complaining ran to the side of the bridge in search of Tristin. "You dummy, they don't have rabbits in this valley! Get back to your post before we get in trouble again."

They may not have caught Tristin but he was in trouble. The raging waters of the river were pulling him hard and he was struggling to keep hold of the side of the bridge. He had to pull himself to shore, he didn't know much about the river but if it was supposed to be worse than the valley, he had no interest in finding out. Slowly, he dug his fingers into the side of the rocks and pulled his body closer to the shore. Then, another flash of lightning crashed into the ground obliterating another tent. Again, the thunder shook the ground, its tremor was so intense that some of the rocks from the bridge shook loose. This caused Tristin to lose his grip on the bridge and instantly the river had him. With what energy he had left he fought to reach the river's edge. His body beaten from fighting the storm he didn't have the strength to fight the currents and the River Onyx claimed another victim.

Chapter 21

The Orc Camp

The bitter cold mountain rain was relentless in its attack on Calembour Valley. The valley, which was thought by the inhabitants of Trubanius as a living thing, contained a conscience that seemed in control of its weather. Although the climate of the valley could change in an instant it hadn't seen this type of rage in over a century. Massive bolts of lightning rained from the sky obliterating everything in its path as its tremendous thunder aftershocks shook the valley to its core, literally tearing it apart. The presence of the immense orcish army and the sheer malice and rage they brought with them had an effect on Calembour that few in the world had ever witnessed.

The Orc Camp

Darius and Keeris darted frantically from tent to tent trying to avoid the random orc guards patrolling the camp. Their bodies were frozen from the rain as they longed to linger by the large orc tents, whose outer skins were warm to the touch due to the large fires inside. The feeling of want for the warmth of the orc fires was quickly eliminated as each lightning strike revealed their surroundings.

The orc tents were immense in size, which was fitting for the sheer size of their battle-laden residents. Stakes protruded from the ground at every tent opening, all containing various sized skulls affixed through the top of each stake. Whether it was an orcish fashion statement or a sense of pride to display their latest kill, it very boldly advised the two young wizards to keep clear of these monsters. Also affixed to the side of every tent was a massive banner. This banner was pure black with the exception of a border that looked like red flames and in the center was the head of a red dragon; its mouth open with teeth bared and its eye reflected the light giving an appearance as if it were watching the two navigate through the camp.

Simply breathing was becoming a chore as Darius and Keeris' lungs burned from the exertions of fighting through the winds and frozen rain all while trudging through the mud created by the downpour.

Neither said a word as they scurried from tent to tent, not wanting to make any noise that would alert the orcs of their existence. The worry in their eyes was enough to tell each other how they felt, both scared of their situation and deeply worried by the absence of their comrade.

Keeris took the lead, running immediately after the illumination of a lightning bolt disappeared or just as a tempest wind cut through the valley. It had been two hours since they had crossed the bridge, the blackness in the sky made it impossible to determine the time or see how close they were to reaching the eastern pass. However, the rage of the storm did have the benefit of keeping the orcs inside their tents which was a gift Darius and Keeris didn't take for granted.

Another bolt of lightning lit up the sky and as soon as the light died away the two ran, trying to control their movements as the ground shook from the consequent thunder. As Keeris rounded the corner of the next tent he crashed full force into a wall that threw him backwards. The blunt force of the collision briefly knocked the breath out of him as he struggled in the mud to regain his composure. As he looked up an instant sense of terror overtook him as Keeris realized that he hadn't hit a wall but the battle-clad armor of a massive orc warrior!

Bending down the two large bright green eyes of the orc stared straight into Keeris' hidden under his wizard cloak. His two large canine teeth on his bottom jaw protruded from his mouth, a large scar cut across his right eye and a large golden ring reflected what little light there was from his left ear. "Looks like mud bunny soup tonight," the orc said with a huge grin. "BOYS, stoke the fire we've got a live one."

"Yfirtep sucimini". The words flew from Keeris' mouth on instinct alone as even he was still dumbstruck at his situation. Instantly the bright green eyes of the orc clouded over to gray as he stopped, petrified in his tracks. A breath of relief quickly followed by both Darius and Keeris until the large orc, frozen like a statue, tipped over. It happened all in an instant and neither Darius nor Keeris could react to stop what happened next. As the orc tipped, he fell straight into the side of a large tent. The wall of the tent tore open, giving way to the orcs massive bulk as if it had been made of paper. As the orc crashed to the ground the contents of the room went flying, along with its soldiers taking refuge inside. Insults and curse words flew across the room as an even larger orc walked across the room, picked up the now petrified orc like a rag doll and called loudly to the others in the room.

"Boys this aints no druken squid, we gotz a wizard en ourz camp! Ring da bell, itz time to HUNT!"

Darius quickly pulled Keeris from the mud. "We have to run, NOW, this will be the first place they look!" Their legs burning from the strain the two ran with everything they had left, no longer waiting and cautiously running from tent to tent. The noise of the warning bell cut through the fierce winds only to be drowned out by the random rolls of thunder. The whole camp was now roused to life and could be heard yelling and cursing as they began their search.

"We can't track verminz with the cursed sky spittin at us! git the hounds!"

It wasn't much later when the ear piercing sound of howling could be heard from the far side of the camp. Along with the screaming and howling of orcs, excited to see some action, caused for some extra motivation to push them even harder to find an exit from the camp.

Another blast of lightning lit up the sky, revealing the location of dozens of orcs scouring the area when Darius suddenly had an idea. In an unnatural sense of clarity, he remembered back to his home in the clearing. Back to a much simpler and safer time when he had only first learned of his quest and the existence of all the true evil in the world. Back when there was only a single spell in his arsenal, a spell that at the time could do little more than start a dry twig on fire. Darius recalled the tent where he and Tristin first practiced for hours and the resulting charred mess after they had been successful. It was this image that chased the fear away and brought a small smirk to Darius' face.

Quickly, Darius grabbed a large plank that had been cast aside in the mud and leaned it against the neighboring orc tent. Using the plank to shield an area of the tent from the torrent rains Darius quietly mouthed the spell "fortia" and quickly grabbed Keeris and pulled him to the next tent.

In a matter of seconds, the tent frame and supports erupted into a blazing fire. Even the frozen rains weren't enough to quell the power behind the young guardian's spell. Darius chuckled as they ran from the tent and Keeris quickly followed cue. In a matter of minutes, Darius and Keeris had a trail of burning tents in their wake. As these tents behind them burned the strong winds started to blow the embers to the adjacent tents. The happy grunting of the orcs was now replaced with furious screaming and cursing as they quickly gave up chase of the wizards and focused on containing the fire.

Then, as suddenly as the furious storm hit

the valley, the winds died down and the rains subsided. The clouds quickly dissipated and the bright and warm sun that had graced the valley just a day ago had suddenly returned. Darius and Keeris had to squint their eyes at the sudden brightness as their pupils readjusted to the light. The cries of the orcs rang out behind them as the still raging fire kept their attention from the wizards.

"Look, Darius!" Keeris grabbed at Darius' sleeve and motioned him to the east. There were only two tents and a short forty-yard gap between them and the trail leading back into the Shemod mountains. "Quickly, quick, quick let's get out of this place while the attention is off us!"

"You don't have to tell me twice". Quickly checking his surroundings Darius followed Keeris and they cautiously ran for the path.

The ground was still thick with mud after the hard rains and although the forty-yard dash to the path wasn't far they still labored to push their bodies. Just as they reached the edge of the path and their spirits were raised up with a clean getaway, their hearts dropped to the pit of their stomachs after a piercing "ARH-WOOOOOOOOOOOOO" cut through the air. Instantly they turned to face their adversaries. Even though the orcs had abandoned pursuit to fight the fire the wolves had the scent of their prey and once they started to track only victory or death would dissuade them.

Saliva dripping from large vampiric teeth, the five wolves' upper lips were curled over in a fierce snarl as they barred their teeth in an angry growl. They stood nearly twice the size of Darius and Keeris, their blackish-blue fur matted down over massive leg muscles. Slowly they advanced on their prey, the largest of the wolves leading the pack while one on each side broke away and began flanking the wizards from either side. The two were backed up against the sheer cliffs on either side of the mountain pass. If they turned to run the wolves would quickly be on top of them, they had to hold their ground.

Eyes darting quickly from one wolf to the next Keeris extended his right arm, "Ecarbme secidar". Vines shot up from the earth like an octopus's tentacle from the water grabbing two of the wolves beside the leader and quickly began entangling them. Squeals of pain and surprise echoed from the two wolves as they unsuccessfully ripped and clawed their way from the vines as the other three wolves remained undaunted and continued their advance.

Darius also joined in the attack with his own magic. As he backed up tightly to the cliffs edge, he held his left palm against the cold stone face and recited a spell from beneath his cloak. "Melog et lapis, ad mativ". Instantly the earth began to shake as the rock surface began to crumble and move. Slowly, the cliffs surface gave way and a large stone golem broke free from the mountain side. Its massive body stood twice the size of the wolves as it lumbered forward.

The two wolves flanking either side sprang forward to attack the stone giant. The first wolf attacked low and attempted to sink its fangs into the stone calf while the second wolf attacked his face and was batted out of the sky by the golems mighty fist. With a loud cry, the wolf flew backwards 20 yards and hit the ground with a thud. The golem then grabbed the second wolf by the back of the neck and threw it across the valley until it hit one of the surrounding tents, tearing through the fabric and disappearing inside.

As the golem turned to face the leader of the wolf pack it was too slow as the large wolf leapt through the air and sunk its razor-sharp teeth straight through its solid rock neck. As the wolf clamped down hard, it bit through the stone and the life left the golem as it crumbled to the ground.

Darius and Keeris were still slowly backing up the mountain pass and away from the scene as the massive wolf fell to the ground in a pile of rubble, shaking the debris from its face and recomposing itself. Then the great blue wolf again affixed its eyes on its prey and again began advancing.

"Well, the vine trick was good, got any other tricks up your sleeve?" Darius' mind was racing, he had trained for this for months but in the heat of the moment he was struggling to find the right spell to take down this monster wolf. Unfortunately, Keeris was in the same predicament. All the reading and training under Theshius was great but it did little to prepare them for the real-life situations they were facing now.

The massive wolves' muscles tightened and its large claws dug deep into the earth. With one powerful lunge, the blue wolf launched its body through the air towards the cowering wizards. At the same moment, Keeris rose an arm and muttered a spell under his breath releasing a blazing light which exploded between them and the wolf. The bright light temporarily blinded the blue wolf; however, its trajectory had already been set in motion as its body hurled straight towards Darius. Unable to cast a spell to deflect the wolf's mass Darius took the full weight of the wolf's bulk.

After several moments the blinding light disappeared and Keeris' eyesight returned. There, lying just feet from him was Darius laying on the rocky path, covered in blood with the great blue wolf laying on top of him. Keeris' hands were quivering, and his voice was broken as he tried to call out to his friend, "Darius? Darius please speak to me!"

A thin stream of blood began running down the mountain pass mixing with the mud pools of the forest floor. Slowly Darius' arm began to twitch from under the wolf. "Darius!" Keeris pushed with all the strength he had left to try and move the wolf's body off of Darius. Slowly the muddy, blood stained grimp pulled his body out from under the wolf's lifeless frame. "What! How? What spell did you use? How, I mean how did you kill it?!" Keeris was excited and confused and just overall happy they were both still alive.

Darius, coughing from the weight that was just released from his body, reached back under the wolf and retrieved a small dagger. "A great wizard gave me this dagger and told me this may help me in times when magic cannot".

"Wow!...... I'm glad he did, mmhhmmm!" Keeris had too many emotions running through his body at the moment. The exhaustion from the day's journey, fear from his run-in with the orcs along with the chase of the wolves, grief when he thought he had lost his friend and happiness that it seemed like it was finally behind them. Keeris couldn't help but release a flood of tears as he embraced Darius with all the remaining strength he could muster. "You're limping, are you sure you're ok?"

Darius wiped away a tear from his cheek, not one of pain but from the contagious emotions Keeris was emitting. "I'll be okay, the weight of the wolf crushing me was a little more than I expected. Do you think maybe you could help me walk for a while? I'd really like to get as far from this orc camp as we can, I don't see much left of the fire so it probably won't be long before they start looking for us again. That and I'm not sure if all of the wolves are dead and I want to get as far from them as we can. Besides that, we need to get to the top of this path and meet up with Tristin"

Keeris grabbed Darius' arm and swung it around his shoulder to help steady some of his weight. Together the two began their ascent up the eastern path, away from the orc army and towards a much larger and dangerous foe; the red dragon.

Chapter 22

The Red Banner

The sun was beginning to set on the Shemod mountain range once again, casting its long shadow across the valley behind them. Darius and Keeris had reached the top of the first peak on the mountain pass and were both ready to collapse from exhaustion. They hadn't stopped moving since the day began and even after their escape from the orcs they hadn't even paused to eat, and the strain of a very taxing day was catching up to them.

"I... can't... go... any further." Kerris dropped to his knees and grabbed his stomach. "I need some food and I need to rest".

"I agree buddy." Darius had also been trying not to concentrate on how badly his own stomach was hurting him. "We won't be able to have a fire up here though I'm afraid. We wouldn't want the light or smoke to attract any unwanted attention".

"No... Nope, not having it!" Keeris rubbed his hands up and down his arms for warmth. The cool air of late autumn mixed with the icy breeze of the mountain winds was too much for him. Momentarily forgetting his fatigue and hunger, the want for warmth pushed Keeris to get back to his feet and begin gathering sticks and twigs from the side of the path.

Darius could only watch as his curiosity got the better of him. Although he hadn't known Keeris very long, this reaction seemed somewhat out of character for him. Did he not understand that a fire would be much more dangerous than fending off the cold? Or, were the events that had taken place today simply too much for him and he needed an outlet? Either way, Darius didn't have the strength to argue, much less stop Keeris from starting a fire.

"Come, come Darius! Come sit with me, it's time for warm food, mmhhmmm!". A half-smile flashed across Keeris' weary face as he urged his friend to sit beside him. He then turned his attention to the stack of lumber he had gathered, placed his hands over it and quietly recited a spell. "Fotia, fotia, fotia occultis aparta."

Darius frowned, his eyebrows narrowed, as a look of confusion filled his face. "Why didn't the spell work?" Was Keeris that tired that he didn't have the strength to cast a simple combustion spell?

Keeris simply smiled and again gestured for his friend to come and sit with him. Slowly, Darius willed his worn body to stand and he slowly made his way over to Keeris. Again, a look of curiosity filled Darius' face, the woodpile was warm! Darius could feel the heat radiating off the pile of sticks but there was no fire! Then all became clear. As Darius took one more step near the camp, he felt his body pass through a magical barrier. Instantly afterward, he could see the fire; he could feel the intense warmth and see the smoke rise ten feet above the flames and disappear into nothing! Keeris had created an invisible barrier around the fire to shield it from any unwanted eyes.

"You're going to have to teach me that one, I can't think of a more perfect time for that spell than now!" Darius let his shoulders fall as he patted his friend on the back and sat down alongside Keeris.

Together the two ate their dinner in silence, vigilantly watching the mountain path. Although neither could bring themselves to say it out loud, they were both anxiously waiting for Tristin to catch up to them.

Slowly, the last remnants of the sun disappeared beyond the western wall of the lower Shemod mountains and the Wall of Bouwind. Bodies tired and broken from a hard day's travel, both Keeris and Darius tipped sideways near the fire and let their fatigue take them as they both drifted off to sleep.

Earlier that same afternoon, from the stronghold at Dragon Rock, another army began to move. This army was an immense collection of the red dragon's followers. This army was of a much different variety than that which left the Chamber of Death less than two days prior. That army was a collection of battle-ready orcs, flying the black banner with pride as they traveled west. Their mission was to destroy the wizard threat by intercepting them in the Calembour Valley. This new army was of a different breed altogether. Massive outpourings from the Lands Below filled the mesa of Dragon Rock. This army was unlike any the world had seen since the Age of Magic had ended three centuries ago.

Drelokh, the mighty red dragon, took to the sky as he looked down on his new army with pride. Although he didn't have the time to train them as battle-hungry warriors, the generations they had spent in Broudin and the tunnels of Bhulek had made them spiteful. The creatures of the underworld hadn't needed the experience of the Lands Above to know they hated all of its inhabitance for taking it from them. This new army flew a blood-red banner. In its center was a large orc shield with dragon claws raked across it and the words "The Reclaiming" written across the bottom. Thousands of these banners flew as their captains barked out orders to start moving, and slowly the army began its march to the east.

On the other side of Trubanius, far to the east of the Shemod Mountains, another military force had taken shape. East of the Vahnulth river and far to the north of the grimp village, near the foothills of Trubanius's second largest mountain range, they had assembled. This was an army seven months in the making. Shortly after Darius and Tristin had left the confines of their village, the villagers led by Heretius and the other guardians of the world began recruiting any and every able-bodied inhabitant of Trubanius.

Tension was in the air as the army, of which they coined themselves the Abovelanders, waited for the arrival of their enemy. With the advantage of the guardians and their Colifiate's in hand, they were able to send ample warning to the Abovelanders of the red dragon's advancements. The Vahnulth river had only two crossing points as the massive river split the world of Trubanius in two. One of these crossings was the mighty bridge west of the small grimp village. That bridge was constructed to support an army along with battle wagons and mighty animals. The crossing to the north was also a well-crafted and sturdy bridge, however, this crossing was only wide enough for roughly four full grown male dwarves to cross shoulder-to-shoulder. The Abovelanders used this military positioning to their advantage. Since they knew the army was on the move and heading towards them, they waited on the eastern border to force the opposing army to thin their ranks while they crossed.

As far to the west as the Abovelanders could see, small curls of smoke began to fill the sky. They were well aware that this was the army they were waiting for. There was a stiffness in their bodies as the fear of what was coming filled each of the dwarves, elves, grimps, colivien, kolerunts and all the creatures waiting to fight. None of them had ever seen or felt the burden of war and the terror that was soon headed their way made them sick with fear.

Chapter 23

The Battle Begins

Tension filled the air as the early rays of the sun reflected off the frost covered ground. The Abovelanders got very little sleep the preceding night as fear of death loomed over them. The previous morning their scouts had spotted the red dragon's army closing in on their position. Now the unease of war was all around them as great billows of smoke engulfed the forest on the opposing side of the bridge. The shouts and cries carried on the wind as the Abovelanders could now hear the approaching army. They were close, there was no turning back now, war would soon be upon them.

General Tae, one of the oldest of the wood elf race, rode back and forth on his white steed shouting words of encouragement to those in the front lines. Tae was one of the few amongst the Abovelanders who had seen the true heat of battle. Three hundred years ago he watched as many of his closest friends were taken from him during the raiding battles of the red dragon's first campaign. When the call of the guardians went out seven months ago, Tae was one of the first to join the cause. His father was one of the first to the order of the Guardians and was killed by Drelokh himself during the final battle of the war. Now, vengeance burned thickly through his blood as revenge for his fallen comrades fueled him to destroy as many of the dragon's followers as he could and cleanse Trubanius of their evil. "Fellow companions and new friends! Soon evil will be upon us, soon those foul creatures of the deep will attempt to cross that bridge! In this day! In this hour! We shall be the protectors of Trubanius! Let us drive these vulgar beings back to the depth from whence they came! Today you not only fight for yourselves, today you fight for all the inhabitance of the lands above! Draw your swords! Ready your bows! Together we will purge this land of hate and misery! Raise your voices and let the enemy know we are here! Raise your voices and let them know we do not fear them! This is our land! WE WILL NOT BACK DOWN!"

As the front lines of the orcs and goblins

broke through into the clearing prior to the bridge they stopped dead in their tracks. The wild cries of the Abovelanders seemed to hit them like a wrecking ball as their own battle cry silenced. The following ranks of the dragon's army slammed into the front lines as they weren't expecting them to stop, causing chaos as they began fighting amongst themselves.

A massive, battle clad, orc pushed his way through the ranks until he had cleared the front lines. This may have been the shortest gap over the Vahnulth yet it was still roughly one hundred yards across. Quickly and silently he scanned the opposing banks and saw his enemies waiting for them. Rolling back his shoulders and facing his head to the sky he let out a blood-curdling scream that echoed throughout the clearing. His eyes were crimson red and his words were filled with hate and disdain, even for his own comrades. "You call yourselves warriors!" The spite filled orc reached down and picked up a goblin by his breastplate. Then as if he were a small sack of potatoes, threw him over the cliff to his death. "Don't back down, don't stop fighting. This land is ours! KILL! SLAUGHTER! DESTROY!"

Immediately scores of creatures poured from the trees and began running across the bridge to fight the Abovelanders.

Unfazed by the onslaught, Tae rode again to

the front of the line, sword raised high. "Archers, nock and draw!" Tae waited patiently as his adversaries scrambled across the bridge. Once the first ranks had reached about three quarters of the way Tae forcibly lowered his sword and yelled "FIRE"!

The battle for Trubanius had officially begun as hundreds of arrows sailed through the sky. Many of the Abovelanders arrows skipped off the side of the stone bridge or sailed wildly into the abyss of the river. Yet, from their ranks, hundreds of wood elves with keen eyes and a natural born proficiency for the bow also let loose a volley of arrows. As each of these arrows met their mark the enemy forces were quickly halted. Dozens of bodies plummeted to the raging waters below while the remainder slowly piled up, turning into an impassable barricade on the bridge. The spirits of the Abovelanders were greatly lifted as they watched their enemy's fall from a safe distance, as the skilled elven archers continued their barrage, picking off the enemy from the opposing bank.

The battle had quickly turned in their favor as the goblin archers attempted to return fire but struggled to propel their arrows over the river's expanse. Cheers rang across the valley as the Abovelanders rang out in cries of victory as they easily held their tactical advantage. However, their shouts of joy were short lived as the next phase of their enemy's advancements began.

Trees began to fall from the forest as heavily armored wagons were dragged to the river's edge. Massive trebuchets were quickly anchored to the ground as orcs began loading the catapults with large spiked boulders. The elven archers quickly tried to disable the trebuchets by attacking the orcs loading them but there were too many and they were too heavily armored.

The same giant orc that had started the battle walked back and forth on the banks calling out orders, screaming at his followers to attack. "Hurry those buckets you maggots! Light the payload and FIRE!" The boulders loaded in the trebuchets sprang to life as the torches touched them, they were instantly ablaze. Only moments later, the latch was released and dozens of flying fireballs hurdled through the sky. A few of the boulders fell short of their mark and smashed into the walls of the canyon, the rest sailed into trees and sent the Abovelanders flying in every direction.

Tae was again rallying his troops. He knew very well the inexperience of his soldiers would cause them to run at the first tide change. "Hold fast! The battle is still ours! Ready the ballista's! Let them feel the sting of our reach!"

The Battle Begins

From the edge of the tree line were two dozen heavily armed ballista's waiting, ready to unleash their fury. Fortunately for the Abovelanders, the battle arena had been chosen weeks ago so they had ample opportunity to battle test their weapons. With a powerful "Whoosh" the massive arrows flew through the air taking out the enemies that were pinned down on the opposing wall. Two of the ballista arrows found their mark on the trebuchets blowing them into splinters. Again, the Abovelanders felt the fuel of the war turning in their favor, they had their enemy pinned back. Quickly, both sides continued to reload and fire their weapons adjusting their trajectory on each volley, while the elven archers continued to pick off any of the red banner army that moved within range.

Angrily, the orc captain pushed his own men into the fray spitting and cursing. "Where are the Bhorks! Clear that path you useless swine!"

The front lines of the red banner army split to allow six riders to break through the ranks. Large creatures with the bodies of giant wolves and squared skulls that looked like battering rams. Two massive lower teeth protruded from their mouths like curved tusks and their bodies were completely covered in armor. On top of each of these creatures was a small goblin rider, equally protected in chainmail. With impressive speed for their size, the six creatures charged the bridge, lowering their heads and slamming them into the fallen red banner warriors casting them off the side of the bridge with little effort. Quickly the elven archers adjusted their aim to stop these beasts from breaking through. Even with well-placed shots, very few arrows found their way between the cracks in the armor and the massive Bhorks continued on. Quickly following suit, the red banner army fell in behind the creatures and again attempted to cross the bridge to reach the Abovelanders who waited nervously for their arrival.

As the first of the Bhorks breached the last of the fallen soldiers a well-placed elven arrow found its mark. Straight through the eye of the massive beast, its face smashed into the stone bridge as its body continued to hurdle forward. Shortly after a second Bhork met the same fate followed by a third, but their time was up as the bridge just wasn't long enough.

Tae patiently waited at the end of the bridge with a large curved scimitar drawn in each hand. The three remaining Bhorks barreled past the bridge and straight for Tae. Nimbly Tae's white stallion jumped to the side of the bulky beast as Tae's sword sliced through the goblin rider. With a massive leap, Tae jumped from his horse and landed on the third Bhork. With one seamless attack, Tae's blade slipped under the goblin's armor slicing his head from his body while his second scimitar pierced straight through the skull of the beast instantly dropping it.

"Hold the line!" With little effort, Tae remounted his steed and charged the bridge. The remaining Bhorks began rampaging through the Abovelanders ranks. They didn't have a massive beast of their own to counter so they were forced to fight with brute force. Many of the elven archers turned their attention from the bridge to silence the riderless beast, while a group of burly dwarves met the second head-on. The Bhorks were quickly subdued, however, they had served their purpose. The Abovelanders attention was pulled from the bridge long enough that their enemy was now nearly upon them.

Without hesitation, Tae kicked his heels into the side of his horse charging down the bridge to meet his foe head-on. He managed to slice through about ten of the leaders until the well aimed swing of a mace crippled the front leg of his horse. With a powerful leap, Tae launched his body into the air landing on the shoulders of a towering ogre. Gracefully he flung both weapons in a downward angle and plunged them into the skull of the ogre. Slowly his massive bulk dropped, the scimitars stuck too deep to retrieve so Tae left them and again dodged forward into the fray. Pulling two large daggers from his waistband he continued to defend the bridge slicing through the surrounding goblins while dodging the volleys of arrows from either side. The bodies again began to pile up on the bridge when a sharp piercing sting struck Tae's side. A goblin dagger was buried to its hilt just under his ribcage. Slowly Tae's eyes met that of the goblin, an upward curl on its lips as its pointed tongue licked the side of his sharp teeth in delight. Tae had gone as far as he could, with a flick of his wrist he flung both daggers straight into the eyes of two nearby orcs, dropping them to their knees. Then, with the last of his breath, he drew the goblin who had stuck him in close, wrapped an arm around his neck and let his body fall from the bridge into the torrent waters below.

First a dozen, then a hundred of the red banner army breached the bridge. The archers tried to hold the remainder at bay while the rest of the army engaged in hand-to-hand combat. Arrows now flew in both directions as the enemy was launching arrows while rushing the bridge and many of the trebuchets that were still operational continued returning volleys. A large ball of fire was launched through the air in a perfect arc hurdling straight for

the largest gathering of elven archers. There was no
time to dodge, even for the nimble elves as they
watched in horror as the massive fireball sailed
toward them. The red banner army had found its
foothold, they had claimed the bridge and the war
was now turning. The Abovelanders did everything
they could to hold off the opposing army but they
were simply outnumbered and outmatched.

The elves dropped to a knee and covered
their faces as the impending blast of the trebuchet
was true to its mark. The elves could feel the
intense heat of the fireball as it closed in and then
hovered above their heads! A look of fear and
astonishment filled their faces. They could nearly
reach up and touch the flaming ball and yet it stopped
as if frozen in time. Then in the next moment, the
ball again hurdled with immense force back in the
direction it had originated from. With a giant blast,
the fireball came back into contact with the
trebuchet that had launched it creating a small
shockwave from the blast, incinerating the catapult
and everyone near it.

The sight of a guardian fighting alongside
them gave the Abovelanders a renewed sense of vigor
as a number of grimps reloaded a ballista and
continued their assault. As a massive arrow let loose
from the ballista, it sailed through the air and

collided with full force into the last remaining trebuchet. The onslaught of the red banner began to slow; their army was still massive in size but their casualties were also great. The Abovelanders loss was relatively minimal, few creatures lost their lives and few more had received any serious injuries during the battle. It again seemed as if, once more, the creatures of the underworld had lost their drive to continue. Even the orc commander's drive to push his warriors into the heat of battle began to wane. The volley of arrows slowed as the creatures of the red banner gave up their advancements on the bridge while the last of the goblin fighters on the east side of the river was struck down by a dwarven blow.

Suddenly, everything was silent. The stench of war filled the air as small mountains of enemy bodies covered the now tarnished and stained bridge. The Abovelanders weren't ready to cry out in victory as their opponent looked on from the west, also not ready to admit their defeat. Minutes passed and no one moved, neither side would turn their backs on their enemies. Then, without warning, a massive shadow covered the Abovelanders as if someone had suddenly blocked out the sun! Wings spread wide the great red dragon circled the woodland forces. Gracefully the dragon pulled his gigantic wings in tight and dove with incredible speed. At the last moment, his great wings again unfurled catching his body like a parachute and gently lowering himself to the ground. A great rush of wind from his wings threw back any of the nearby Abovelanders as the dragon touched the ground. Drelokh didn't waste time with words, a fierce twinkle in his eye was all that preceded his attack. With a deep rumble inside his chest that could be felt like a minor earthquake, he wrenched back his neck, opened his mouth and let fly an incinerating blast of heat and fire. Those closest to the blast were instantly engulfed in flames and their bodies turned to ash.

In the next instant, the inferno crashed with full force into a great wall of ice. Two of the guardians combined their abilities to deflect the powerful dragon's breath before it could claim any more victims. With a vengeful sneer, the dragon again reeled back and released another blast of fire, this time blasting through the wall of ice and sending the Abovelanders flying in all directions. Powerful cheers were heard from the western bank as the creatures of the red banner watched their leader decimate his foes. Yet, not one was fearless enough to attempt to renew the attack, when the red dragon was enraged there was no guarantee that he would distinguish between ally and foe in his assault.

The dragon was relentless in his attack. The archers attempted to slow his siege but their arrows haplessly bounced off the dragon's thick scales. The few guardians within the Abovelanders ranks did little to dispel the dragon's fiery breath, with each attack their defenses dwindled.

Again, the mighty dragon lifted his neck high into the air as another barrage built up within his chest. As Drelokh opened his mouth to release another blast another great shadow cast across the valley. Drelokh's attention was momentarily pulled from the battle as he glanced at the shadow above. An instant later the large silhouette in the sky dropped with the speed of a bullet and crashed headlong into the red dragon.

The collision was like a shockwave and the few remaining Abovelanders that were still standing were thrown to the ground. The bodies of the two great dragons rolled backward on top of the large stone bridge. Erquein had his claws wrapped tightly around Drelokh's throat. "It's been a long time my old friend."

Before Erquein could continue his assault, he could hear the powerful pops and cracks of the stone and concrete below them. Suddenly the support of the large bridge gave way and the two dragons plummeted down towards the torrent waters of the Vahnulth.

Moments later the two beasts flashed into the sky, flying parallel to each other slashing and clawing at each other like angry wolves. Both armies' eyes were affixed to the sky, watching a powerful sight rarely witnessed. Great blasts of fire illuminated the sky as Erquein and Drelokh would release, circle around and crash their bodies back into each other. The battle seemed to carry on for hours in the sky while not a moment of time passed below. Scales rained down from the sky as the dragons ripped, bit and tore into each other. Drelokh was a larger, more powerful dragon than Erquein, however, he struggled to match the speed and agility of his adversary.

In a nimble turn, Erquien swiftly maneuvered past Drelokh fire blast and sunk his teeth deep in Drelokh's throat while simultaneously raking his claws across the red dragon's chest. With a deep and powerful cry, the red dragon's pain could be felt across Trubanius. In a rage of adrenaline, Drelokh tore Erquein's teeth from his neck and returned the blow tearing through the skin of his wings and engulfing him in fire.

With little life left, Erquein began to fall from the sky, his wing broken he tried to slow his descent as his body crashed into the remaining structure of the stone bridge and then disappeared into the torrent waters of the Vahnulth. The red dragon had nothing left to enjoy his victory. He too had received a near-fatal blow and slowly and painfully he retreated west, back towards the Shemod mountains.

The creatures of the red banner and the Abovelanders stared at each other from across the chasm. With the bridge now fully destroyed there was no way for either side to continue the attack, bringing with it an end to the first battle of the new age.

Chapter 24

Dragon Rock

Keeris woke painfully, the nights of sleeping on the hard ground were taking its toll on him. The crisp mountain air had caused him to lose feeling in the tips of his fingers and toes as his fire had died away during the night. Slowly he willed his body to stand as he staggered around the campsite, collecting more fuel for his fire. The need for a warm breakfast was all the persuasion he needed to keep his legs moving.

Darius on the other hand had become very accustomed to sleeping on the ground, as well as in the outdoors. As opposed to Keeris and Tristin, who'd spent their summer training with Theshius, while sleeping in soft beds in the hidden swamp gate he'd spent his nights outdoors, sleeping in the dirt or hidden in trees. The pleasant smells of roasting meat pulled Darius from his sleep coma. He had only known Keeris a couple of days but he was already wondering how he survived the wilds without Keeris' cooking.

"He's not here". Keeris was typically always so lighthearted and happily living in the moment. However, either from the battle through the orc camp the day before, or the disappearance of his closest friend, Keeris was more solemn than he had been since starting this journey with Tristin.

Darius didn't know how to respond. They both knew deep down after they had gotten separated there was little chance they would all regroup, especially this early. Even if Tristin was still alive it would be extremely difficult for him to follow them through the mayhem they had created in the orc camp. "We, have to hold hope. Tristin has been through so much this past year, and he's now a full-fledged guardian. It's going to take more than that to keep the three of us apart indefinitely!" Darius tried to mask his fear with a smile, but wasn't doing anything to fool Keeris. "We can't afford to wait though. We don't know if the orcs will backtrack and try to follow us and we still have a mission we must finish. I'm sure Tristin will do everything he can to catch up."

The rest of their breakfast was quiet, they both had so much to say but couldn't bring themselves to discuss their missing friend further. After they finished eating, Keeris quickly packed up his supplies and hurriedly disrupted their campsite so anyone following them wouldn't see that anyone had recently stopped here.

Keeris quickly ran back to the path to catch up to Darius who had his Colifiate open and was intently reading. "Hey Keeris, have you read any of this yet this morning?" Darius looked up, wide-eyed, glancing in Keeris' direction who was shaking his head no with his shoulders shrugged. "It sounds like my village has joined forces with yours along with the wood elves, Rewick dwarves and a ton of others! They are making a stand just east of the Vahnulth and expect the dragons Red Banner army to meet up with them in just over a day's time! Sounds like Oliphius has been spying on the dragon's army and updating Heretius on their movements."

Keeris and Darius began hiking down the mountain path while discussing these new events. "Darius, do you... do, do you think they stand a chance? Our people, my people, your people, they can't fight!"

"Well... keep in mind they likely have a couple of guardians on their side. Also, keep in mind their camped on the opposite side of the Vahnulth! Even at the smaller northern pass, the red banner army is going to have a hard time advancing. They will have to greatly thin their army to cross the bridge and that's going to make them sitting ducks with the elves on our side!"

Keeris seemed happy with Darius' explanation and an old familiar smile found its way back to his face. The two young wizards had another long day ahead of them, which passed uneventfully. They traveled for the first half of their day along the mountain pass when they reached a split in the road. One path banked south, remaining in the lower mountains of the Shemod range while the northern pass quickly climbed in elevation, scaling the mighty Dragon Rock. They both knew exactly which path they needed to take but both hesitated slightly. The road north was undoubtedly going to be the most difficult part of their journey. If they continued north, they would reach the top of the massive mesa by nightfall, the home of the red dragon himself.

"Darius, Darius!" Keeris was breathing heavily as the two continued to climb the steep embankment of the mountain. "I've been wondering. Why is it that the guardians don't all get together and take the red dragon on together, together? Shouldn't they be able to, able to take him down with all their power, mmhhmmm?"

"You don't know? I guess I just assumed Theshius would have told you both that!" Darius rubbed his thighs as they began to burn from the climb. "A long, long time ago back during the last battle of the Age of Magic. It was moments after the guardians of the time had cast their spell on the red dragon trapping him. During that brief moment as the dragon was being frozen, as he swore his revenge on everyone in Trubanius, he also cast an evil curse on the guardians. With his last breath the red dragon used some old and dark magic, even the guardians of the time, as powerful as they were couldn't have anticipated it. The curse prevents a magician from, well basically killing the same individual twice. It sounds odd but since the guardians trapped him in what should have been an eternal tomb his dark magic will stop them from ever directly attacking him again."

"Wait, what, really!" Keeris stopped walking for a moment as he processed this information. "Why, why didn't anyone tell Tristin or me" He then looked down at his feet while he continued to climb. "That explains so much!"

The two again continued to climb as the cold mountain winds continued to cut through them. They were higher now than the rest of the Shemod peaks, so the mountain chill was unrestricted as it swirled around Dragon Rock. The hours passed and finally, the grueling climb began to ease as the mountain pass began to level off. Darius and Keeris found themselves at the top of Dragon Rock.

The enormous mesa was a flat peak that continued onward as far as the two could see. The landscape was completely barren with only a few small snow-covered patches and contained no vegetation or wildlife. The young wizards were quickly reminded of the Calembour Valley as they both wondered what shelter they were going to find for their camp.

"Darius..." Keeris slowly turned his body around while he scanned the landscape. "We'll be, we'll be sitting ducks up here if we make camp! Even if we don't, don't stop we're still sitting ducks up here, mmhhmmm."

"I'm guessing that's all part of the reason they chose this spot for their base." Darius threw an arm around Keeris' shoulder and urged him to keep moving. It always brought a smile to Darius as he watched Keeris, always such a positive attitude and his stuttering quirk when he got overly excited. "You know what though, since we already snuck past the

Black Banner army to the west and our villages are about to engage in battle with the Red Banner army to the east, I'm wondering if there's even anyone left behind to defend their keep. We may just be in the most dangerous place in all of Trubanius and still be the furthest from any real danger!" The smile on Darius' face quickly faded as he thought about what truly lay ahead of them. "That is, assuming the dragon isn't home."

The two pushed on long after the sunset behind the Shemod peeks. With what little warmth the sun brought with it now gone, Darius and Keeris pulled their cloaks tightly around their bodies to try and keep in what body heat they still had. A major decision was now laid in front of them. In the distance, roughly another hour's walk ahead of them was a large, black stone structure. They knew all too well this was the entrance to the Chamber of Death. What they didn't know was that the decision they would make next would ultimately decide the fate for all of Trubanius.

"I think we need to use the cover of night and hope the element of surprise is on our side. We shouldn't let this opportunity pass us by!" Darius had always been the strongest strategist of the three and felt very strongly about his plan.

"D-d-d-darius, its-s s-s-ooo cccold up heeere." Keeris tried to rub the cold out of his arms but the past few hours in the cold winds without cover had taken their toll on him. "I, w-want to g-get out of this c-cold so badly. H-however, we are c-cold and tired and it w-would be a m-mistake to try and at-t-tack right n-now."

"It could be very dangerous to sleep up here without protection." Darius thought long and hard about the decision. Deep down he knew Keeris was right about them both needing to recharge before they confronted the dragon. He just hated to give up this opportunity, however in the end the look on poor Keeris' chattering face helped make the decision an easy one. "Alright buddy, I have some wood left in my pack that I grabbed before we left this morning. If you can use that spell from last night to shield our fire, I think we can get a few hours of sleep and try and move on the chamber before dawn."

Quickly agreeing, Keeris quickly knelt by the firewood and began reciting his spell between his chattering teeth. Aside from the gentle arctic breeze, which was fortunately blocked out by Keeris' spell, the mesa was eerily quiet. Nothing stirred as the two wrestled to shut their minds off so they could get a few hours' sleep before quite possibly the biggest day of their lives.

Chapter 25

Chamber of Death

The sky was still dark and the moon still hung low in the sky. Darius rolled to his side and forced his eyes open. Even though his body was exhausted from the climb, his mind wouldn't allow him a relaxing sleep. In the back of his thoughts, he could feel the entrance to the Chamber of Death looming over them and the enduring feeling that they were being watched was too much to allow him a peaceful slumber. Still, for as hard as it was for Darius to rest his friend didn't seem to be sharing in his struggles. It hadn't taken Keeris more than a few moments for sleep to overtake him as he now lies contorted in the dirt, mouth wide open and drool running down his cheek.

Darius giggled slightly at the sight of Keeris, which quickly faded away. He hated to wake Keeris from his sleep so early, but deep down he feared waiting until after the sun had risen to make their move. For just a few hundred yards from where they camped, their final objective lay waiting for them. They were sitting at the doorway to the most feared villain in Trubanius and they were cold, alone, and utterly unprepared. They came all this way and still, they didn't have a solid plan, and that may have been Darius' greatest fear. So much had happened this year and yet it would all soon be in vain if they couldn't think their way past an immortal being, centuries wiser and a hundred times more powerful than they were.

Darius knew he had quite some time before sunrise, so quietly, he pulled his Colifiate from his pack and began to write.

My fellow guardians. Keeris and I are sitting at the entrance to the Chamber of Death and are desperately in need of anyone's advice. We are so close to our goal, yet now that the moment is nearly upon us, we have no idea what to do next! The dragon is just steps away, we've trained for this reason solely, and yet we don't know how to destroy *him. Every scenario I've played in my mind finds us at the same outcome, none of which are in our favor. Please, anyone, we need guidance. I beg you!*

Darius waited and watched his book, longing for a response. He really didn't know what he and Keeris would do next. They could never abandon their quest, but still, was it wise to dive headlong into danger without even a basic plan? The minutes ticked by and Darius began to lose hope. Deep down he knew his fellow guardians were preparing for a massive war and his problems probably weren't their top concern at the moment. Then, suddenly words began appearing in his book.

Darius my friend, I'm very glad to hear you are still well! There has been a terrible weight on my heart every day since the one I asked you to leave our small village, and yet I could never express just how proud of you I am. In this short amount of time you have surpassed all of our expectations and have quickly grown into a powerful young wizard. I truly wish I could give you the key to this battle, unfortunately, none of us still alive know the answer to your question. However, don't be discouraged and don't lose hope for you are more prepared for this battle than you could possibly imagine. The red dragon has a weakness, though I don't believe he knows it, or possibly he simply denies it. You my young friend are that weakness! You, Keeris and Tristin! You are the bright light that will shine through his darkness!

Deep within yourself is the key to defeating his evil! This is the most basic principle of our magic, there cannot be a dark without a light and the greater that darkness, in turn the greater the light. The red dragon knows that your light can outshine his darkness! If you doubt my words ask yourself, why would he send a legion of battle hungry orcs to capture 3 fledgling wizards in the Calembour Valley? The truth is, he fears your power! Do not let his darkness overshadow you! Be brave, be the grimp that gave up his entire life to save his village without a thought for his own protection! You think it a mere coincidence that you were chosen for this task? The blood of dragons runs through your veins! My greatest regret is all the time we had together, and all the time I could have taught and prepared you for this moment, unfortunately in my weakness and ignorance, I failed to see the inevitable future unfold. You think you're small? You think you're weak? I'll tell you one more time, in your heart beats a warrior, in your veins courses a power passed on from generation to generation! The three of you have the light within you. LET YOUR LIGHT SHINE BRIGHT! Hurry home to us, your village misses you dearly and will be fighting this day in your honor. Good luck my friend!

Darius couldn't help but stare at the words in his book. So many emotions were flowing through him. It had been so long since he had allowed himself to think about his family and friends back home, those days seemed like nothing more than a distant dream. Then there was Heretius, there was no one in all of Trubanius whom he had more reverence for, so to read the great praise they had received from him was a bit much for Darius to hold in. Heretius would never steer them wrong and his words so powerfully believed that they could beat the dragon. Still, Heretius mentioned the three of them. It was a stretch early on to think they could accomplish such a feat, and now they were without Tristin. Would Heretius still urge him and Keeris to attack without Tristin?

"No, I can't keep doubting myself and my friends!" Darius stood up with a sense of determination, put his book away and walked over to wake his friend. "Buddy, it's time to get up, we need to move while it's still dark!"

Keeris' voice sounded slightly pinched as his face was partly smooshed into the ground. "I'm awake, I've been awake! You read out loud when you get excited!" Keeris used his sleeve to wipe the drool from his chin and then began to rub his eyes awake, while continuing to talk through a long yawn. "Can't we just blow, blow up the rock and cause a cave in? I really don't, don't want to go in there!"

Darius shook his head, smiling. "Get up buddy!" as he pulled Keeris to his feet. Together they finished the short hike to the massive opening in the side of the chamber. They had been through so much and had walked such a long way yet these next few steps seemed to be the most difficult. Keeris reached down and put his hand on Darius' hand, took a deep breath and lightly pulled Darius down the steps leading into the Chamber.

The entry stairs were slightly illuminated by a faint light reflecting from the rock walls. The stairs themselves took Darius and Keeris down about fifty feet underground until the stairwell opened up into a massive underground chamber. The room itself was huge, the two guardians were shocked that such a structure could exist within the mountain. Darius guessed the room must be at least five hundred feet long and equally wide with torches placed every fifteen feet. Four enormous columns that looked like ancient stone trees helped support the ceiling twenty feet above them.

Keeris was already longing for the cold mountain air, the stench of the underground cavern was overly reminiscent of the days he and Tristin spent in the tunnels under the swamps. It was all too obvious that this hall was very recently in heavy use, a thought that made both of the guardians happy it was empty now.

Darius took a low deep breath to settle his nerves and began to cross the large room, he knew they still had a mission and a dragon shouldn't be too hard to find underground. Yet, before he could take his third step, he could feel the tight grip of a hand holding him back. Slowly turning around, Darius was met by a dark hood and a black face. His heart skipped a beat and fortunately, his words were stuck in his throat as he instinctively wanted to scream. However, in the following moment, he quickly pieced together the puzzle surrounding him. The silhouetted figure was merely Keeris holding him back, but why was he cloaked if they were alone? From within the enveloping darkness of his hood, Keeris was holding up a single finger while slowly shaking his head back and forth. At that instant, Darius then knew they weren't alone as he too had found himself protected by his own guardian's cloak.

Again, turning to face the rear of the room, Darius for the first time saw what had held Keeris back. On the far back wall, on top of a slightly raised surface that appeared to be some sort of stone stage, stood another cloaked figure. Clad entirely in red, his cloak had the appearance of scales as the flickering light of the torches danced off its many surfaces. Whether it was a hint at the creature beneath or part of the cloak itself, two large curved horns protruded from his skull and the serpentine eyes of a dragon were embroidered into the fabric. His hood, like that of a guardian, hid his features completely giving Darius and Keeris no hints as to whom or what they were about to face off with.

Keeris once again pulled on Darius, only this time to urge him forward to confront their likely foe. Slowly they crossed the huge room as their adversary did the same, they met in the center stopping about ten feet from each other.

After a long and somewhat awkward period of silence, the creature in the red cloak spoke. His voice, deep and raspy, had a somewhat slithering sound as he let his S's linger in each word.

"Well met my brothersss. You did well to make it passst the black banner, granted you're one ssshort and had to sssneak past inssstead of fight! The mighty red dragon would like me to welcome you to hisss lair and offer you sssanctuary."

Darius was expecting a full-on attack, yet his words felt like they were doing a better job knocking him off his balance. "What do you mean sanctuary? Sanctuary from what exactly, and where is the dragon and why isn't he telling us this himself?"

"Ssso full of anger! The sssanctuary we offer isss that of peace, protection from thisss war which isss already nearing itss end. Join usss, your powersss would be bessst ssserved the dragon than the grave! Alssso, to anssswer your sssecond quessstion, my liege isssn't currently with usss. He isss quelling a sssmall uprisssing to the eassst and ssshould return momentarily."

Keeris could feel his own nails digging into his skin as he clenched his hand in absolute hatred. "That small uprising is our friends and our family! If you think we would ever turn our backs on our own people and let this world turn to darkness you're greatly mistaken! Even if we lose our lives to you or your dragon, the people of Trubanius won't so easily give in to your hate. We've stopped you once before and it won't be any different this time!"

Darius wanted to grab ahold of his friend and hug him tightly. Throughout the journey they had shared as well as the numerous stories he and Tristin had told him, Keeris had always suffered from a slight stutter, always repeating words as he spoke. Only now, at the end of everything, in the heat of the final moments of battle did his words flow with full strength and conviction. Darius found himself oddly at peace knowing he had the powerful backing of a great friend at his side.

"Ssso foolisssh! I, the all-powerful Audric, captain of the red dragonsss forcesss offer you sssolitude with usss and you ssscoff at our great generosssity. You will now feel that sssting of magic, hundredsss of yearsss beyond your abilitiesss."

"Pluma nigrum circulus ignisss." Audric quickly

swirled his arms in a massive circle while flames erupted from his fingertips. Moments later a fierce ring of fire was surrounding the three of them. Darius and Keeris could feel the intense heat on their hands and were both suddenly very grateful at that moment for the magic of their cloak's protection.

Keeris, still enraged by Audric's taunt to join them as their families perished, didn't wait for a second attack. "Gelida inspiratione glacies!" Keeris had never been as deft at fire magic as his guardian brothers however, he had always been able to surpass Tristin with ice magic. Like the breath of a blizzard, icy veins shot from Keeris and hit Audric head-on encasing him in a frozen tomb of ice.

"Don't let up! He's coming!" Darius yelled to Keeris as the translucent blue ice tomb began to grow crimson. Then in an echoing explosion, Audric blasted from the ice sending icicle shards sailing in every direction. Quickly Darius threw up his left hand while sweeping his right from the ground towards the ceiling. Instantly a wall of stone shot up from the ground like a rock shield protecting them from the blast. In the next moment Darius pushed the wall of stone like a tidal wave crashing down on Audric. However, as the stone wave crashed into him it melted away into a sheet of water, soaking him to the core but preventing any real damage. As the water hit the ground it splashed in every direction making contact with the firewall hissing and instantly turning to steam.

Suddenly the room was a thick foggy haze. Darius knew he was standing next to Keeris but could no longer see him, and worse yet he had no idea where Audric was! The moisture on Darius' hands began to freeze as the haze in front of him slowly turned to glass. However, this wasn't glass! The water vapors in the room were all turning to ice and slowly freezing, entrapping the entire chamber. Darius instantly knew this was Keeris's magic, but what was he planning as now all three of them were trapped?

It was as if time had stopped in the massive chamber. Unable to move, Darius could only watch as the thick fog of the room turned translucent and gradually everything became perfectly clear. The three figures in the room looked like models on display, all frozen in time. Darius could now see how dangerously close Audric had come to attacking Keeris while hidden in the mist. The hood of his cloak was thrown back revealing the face of a lizard, the scales on his skin resembled those on his cloak. Two curved horns protruded from the side of his head and the same yellow slitted eyes that could be seen from beneath the cloak seemed amplified and filled with hate and despair. Audric's arms were held high above his head as he wielded a large broadsword, which was moments from crashing down on Keeris.

The only disruption to this crystal-clear ice stage was the fog that still lingered from Keeris's breath as he never stopped muttering his spell. Then as slowly as the flawlessly clear ice formed the shards around Audric began to turn bright white, burning him with intense cold. Whether Keeris was fully aware of his situation or by sheer luck Audric could feel the strength being sucked out of him. His race had always survived deep in Broudin near the underground lava pits, where his amphibious, cold-blooded, heritage could thrive in the intense heat. Now the penetrating cold was quietly killing him from the inside.

Then the entire chamber began to shake with the deep tremors of a terrible earthquake. Large chunks of rock began breaking from the ceiling and crashing down on the ice tomb while all around Darius and Keeris large cracks began to form in the ice until the entire room shattered. As suddenly as the shocks began, they instantly quelled as all three wizards were dropped to their knees.

Audric, using his sword as a crutch pulled himself back to his feet. The intense yellow in his eyes began to fade, replaced by deep crimson, as the veins in his neck began to pulsate from his body. "I may have underessstimated your ssstrength, but thisss all endsss now! You had your chance for sssurvival, now I will have the honorsss of killing hisss majesssty's rival. Now DIE!"

Audric held his sword solidly in his right hand while slowly running his left along the blade. As his hand slid along the metal it instantly transformed the steel into a dazzling blue flame. He then hesitated for only a moment as he held his sword vertically in front of himself while saluting his adversaries. The next instant he sprang to life, throwing his body towards the guardians.

Neither Keeris nor Darius were trained in hand-to-hand combat as they awkwardly tried to defend against the onslaught. Keeris didn't have a weapon of his own so quickly created a shield of light while Darius used a similar method and attempted to parry with his small dagger. The battle was quick and one-sided. Audric was simply too powerful and with a few deft moves from his blade he cut through Keeris' shield, the force of the impact throwing his body across the room until he slammed into a stone pillar. Keeris dropped unconscious to the ground as a small stream of blood ran down his face. Audric then turned his attention to Darius, with a quick and powerful swing of his sword he dislodged the dagger from Darius' hand sending it sailing across the room. Then with a second powerful swing, he cracked through the magical shield in Darius' left arm dropping him to his knees. They were simply no match for the reptilian wizard as he hovered over Darius his sword raised for the strike.

"A few more yearsss and you may have made a formal adversssssary. However, thisss isss where your ssstory endsss!" Audric used both hands to bring his fiery blade down on Darius, whom was defeated and defenseless. As the beautiful blue arc of the sword traveled through the air in one final swing the deep crimson color of Audric's eyes slowly faded back to a bright yellow, which in turn slowly faded to black. As Darius looked up at the sword traveling towards him, unable to counter he noticed a second blue light flash across his vision. Just as the sword had come nearly horizontal to the ground a bright blue arrow of pure blue light pierced Auric through the chest and continued on toward the back of the chamber. As the light left Audrics eyes he slowly stumbled backward, his mind racing trying to figure out where he went wrong. As the strength in his hands failed him, he let his sword, now a simple piece of steel again, fall from his grip hitting the floor with a loud echoing clang. Then as his body fell, he caught sight of another silhouetted creature, one he had failed to notice all this time off in the shadows.

Chapter 26

Reunion

Darius couldn't move, he couldn't even think as his brain was swirling trying to piece together the final moments and what actually just happened. He was utterly defeated and his life was forfeit as his enemies' blade was mere inches from cutting through him, then suddenly it all changed. Just a few paces away, Audric the leader of the red dragon's army, now lay lifeless before him and his comrade Keeris was also knocked out against a stone pillar, hopefully still alive and merely unconscious. As Darius attempted to put the puzzle together, he then noticed the same silhouetted creature, the last thing Audric saw before he fell, coming towards him. Darius couldn't make out any details in the low light of the cavern, he could only hope that this mysterious being must be an ally since he saved his life.

Halfway to Darius, the creature abruptly stopped, then nearly sprinted towards Keeris. Darius didn't know what to do next as he slowly pulled his body off the stone floor. He was now on his own again and the thought of solitude didn't sit well as he watched his friend lay unmoving on the ground, with an unknown creature hovering over him. Darius was both physically and mentally drained from their last battle and at the moment could do nothing other than watch the next moments unfurl.

Slowly Keeris was pulled to his feet, visibly shaken but standing on his own strength. Darius watched as the two stood face to face and in the next moment, Keeris threw his body at the other figure, throwing his arms wildly around him, holding him tightly. Darius lost all control of his body as he fell to his knees, tears flowing down his face. His emotions had taken full control and his body tremored while he tried to breathe through his uncontrollable weeping. Through his tears he watched both cloaks fade away as both Keeris and Tristin walked towards him, holding each other tightly.

"I'm glad I caught up to you two!" Tristin helped Darius back to his feet and the two embraced each other tightly.

After wiping the tears of happiness from his face with his sleeves, Darius held Tristin an arm's length away and looked him straight in the eyes. "That's twice now we've been separated on this journey, that won't happen again!" Hugging Tristin one more time, his brain finally started catching up to their situation. "What happened to you back in Calembour Valley and how did you get here? When did you get here?"

The smile slowly melted from Tristin's face and he looked back and forth from Keeris to Darius. "My story is going to have to be one for another day. I've been following the battle out east through my Colifiate and Drelokh is heading this way! We don't have much time to prepare but I can tell you this much. There were few casualties in the battle but it's far from over, the two sides got separated when the bridge was destroyed and now they are likely to meet again in a day's time at Tay's Crossing near our home. Drelokh and Erquein fought and Erquein fell." Tristin could see the worried look in his friend's eyes at this news, but continued on. "I do know that Erquein dealt the red dragon a very serious blow in the battle, bad enough that he retreated to the west. My only guess is that he is coming back here to rest and heal. He could be here at any moment so we will need to have a plan. He may be wounded but I doubt that will make him any less of a danger, in fact he might be more wild and deadly in this state."

Keeris looked back and forth between his friends. "This mountain is massive! If he's hauled up somewhere, we might have a hard time finding him now."

Darius joined in the discussion. "True, but keep in mind he's a dragon! He is way too big to hide, there has to be some pretty large caverns in here that we can follow. He couldn't have come in the entrance we came down, that stairway didn't seem big enough for a full sized dragon?"

Tristin kneeled down next to Audric's body verifying that he was truly dead. After that, he picked up the fallen sword, spinning it slowly in his hand. "The tunnels I took to find you guys definitely weren't large enough for a dragon either. I think Darius is right, we should start searching, there has to be a large passageway through here somewhere."

"Hey guys," Keeris pulled his friends in close. "I realize Drelokh will likely be able to hear us from a mile away, but we should still try and be as quiet and stealthy down here as possible. We really don't know who or WHAT else could be hiding in these tunnels. I'd rather not have a run-in with another group of orcs while searching for a dragon."

The group agreed that keeping quiet was the

best course, but not completely, they would still need to iron out a plan as they searched for the dragon. Finding a dragon sized tunnel proved to be much simpler than any of them would have thought. Near the back of the chamber, just to the right of the stone stage was a large, dimly lit tunnel leading deeper into the heart of the mountain.

Not much was said while the trio carried on. The idea of a plan was intriguing but in the end, none of them had any clue what they could do against the power of a dragon. Tristin and Darius talked about the message that Heretius had left for their group in the Colifiate. Tristin had only seen the message minutes before finding a secret tunnel leading into the chamber and apologized to both Keeris and Darius for not letting them know he was alright. "It never crossed my mind that I could have let you guys know where I was and what happened. How stupid, I'm so sorry for making you both worry!"

"It's okay buddy, you're safe and we're back together again! It's a good thing too since it's going to take the three of us to stand a chance in this!" Keeris seemed back to his normal self again. Fortunately, the gash he received from being thrown into the stone pillar was simply a surface wound and didn't seem to affect him as they traveled.

The hours slowly passed as the three traveled

deeper and deeper into the mountain. Steadily the path seemed to descend deeper and deeper as they traveled, pushing them hundreds of feet below the surface. The tunnel itself held its shape well. Fortunately, a tunnel made for a dragon to travel allowed the three guardians to comfortably walk side-by-side.

It wasn't until after their fourth hour in the gloomy tunnels that Keeris quickly pulled his friends in close and whispered as softly as he could yet still remain audible. "Guys, can you feel that? There's a breeze coming down the tunnel!"

Darius and Tristin stopped and patiently waited. They were nowhere near as sensitive to the world around them as Keeris was. He had spent his life in the trees, reading the forest and using his heightened senses for survival. After a few minutes of pure silence, a subtle breeze made its way through the tunnel and was just strong enough for the grimps to feel it move through the hair on their arms. Their eyes locked on each other; they knew they were close to the end of the tunnel. If Drelokh was seeking refuge near Dragon Rock there was a very good chance he was just ahead!

Again, they continued on, this time making sure to move as stealthily as possible, controlling their steps as they let their feet softly touch the rocky surface. The odds of sneaking up on a dragon were impossibly small, yet they didn't need to draw more attention to themselves than was necessary.

The breeze was much more prominent now, the arctic chill of the mountain air once again began to bite at their skin, lowering their body temperature. Deep down all three of the guardians wanted to create a fire to keep themselves warm but all knew it wasn't worth the risk. They could see the light at the end of the tunnel, a light that was all too symbolically like their journey thus far. Consciously, each of the guardians let their cloaks cover their bodies as they pushed through to the end.

A familiar feeling of the ground shaking once again stopped the guardians dead in their tracks. The bright blue light that had once been a visible sign of their exit was suddenly covered. The swirl of dragon fire licked the walls of the tunnel as it traveled at extreme speeds towards them.

Darius jumped in front; arms extended while placing his palms facing the fire as if he were ready to catch it. "Sol clypeus," Darius cried out as a large translucent shield appeared before him.

As the dragon fire hit the shield it was quickly deflected around the guardians. They could feel the intense heat of the fire, which burned ten times hotter than that of Audric's fire ring. If not for the protection of the cloaks the three would have melted under the unnatural heat, even with Darius' shield guarding them.

After thirty seconds the fire subsided and the cold breeze of the mountain air again filled the large tunnel. Like a low growl, the red dragon's deep and terrifying voice addressed his visitors. "Foolish little guardians! Keep your voices low, I can still hear you! Don't talk at all and I can still smell you!" After another short pause, the red dragon voice grew in magnitude, reverberating off the walls. "Audric! Rid me of these bothersome maggots!"

"Your commander isn't going to come to your aid Drelokh!" Tristin called down the tunnel, almost taunting the great dragon.

There was a brief pause as they waited for the dragon's response. Would he attack them in a fury for killing his top officer or simply not believe them? "So little guardian, you've found a way to best my commander. Not only that, but you've uncovered a name I haven't heard in hundreds of years. How resilient of you! I'm surmounting you've talked with old Erquein? It may trouble you to hear that I've killed him not but a few hours ago. Now come here so I can see the wizards who've learned my past name before I end your short lives."

His scales were a deep black, yet as the sun reflected off its surfaces it appeared to be a deep blood red, and this is why Drelokh became known simply as the red dragon. His upper teeth protruded over his bottom jaw, large whiskers crowned his upper lip and curved around the side of his face. Two immense horns, similar to those of Audric's, projected from the back of his skull and curled backward following the spikes down his spine.

It was then the three guardians caught sight of the wound Drelokh had received earlier that morning while battling Erquein! If not for the reflection of the midday sun against his armored body the wound would have simply been camouflaged by his blood red scales. However, now that the guardians had settled themselves and fully realized their situation did they notice how unsettled the dragon really was. Two steady streams of blood flowed down the red dragon's neck from two gaping puncture wounds, collecting in a small pool beneath where Drelokh rested. Then, along his side, underneath his left wing were three immense claw marks. This was Erquein's final gift to Drelokh in their recent battle as he raked his claws deep, cutting through his scaly defenses, leaving a gas the dragon's side nearly fifteen feet long! Dr may have claimed victory in that battle, how his current state, he didn't look prepared another fight. That would also explain why he called for his commander when he caught wind of the guardians; for in truth his senses were weakened in that he almost missed hearing the guardians advancing down the corridor.

Darius knew the evils that Drelokh had committed, however struggled to bring himself to attack a gravely weekend foe. "Drelokh, you're in no shape to fight us! Don't you think it's time to give up this foolish uprising? Can't we end this war before anyone else has to forfeit their life for this cause?

The fires within Drelokh throat stoked hot as his eyes pierced deep into Darius. "Foolish little grimp! Yes, your stench gives you away! If you think there is any chance I could be bested by your lowly race a second time you're gravely mistaken. Your meek little bodies will soon be crushed beneath my talons. Don't worry though, I'm a generous ruler and I will happily return your bodies home as I drop your carcasses from the sky onto your village."

There was obvious distress in the dragon's physique as he pulled his body to his full form. A slight tremor pulsated through Drelokh's body as he stretched his chest muscles, blood continuing to run down his muscular leg.   Smoke began billowing from the dragon's nostrils as the fire in his throat gathered, preparing for a second attack.

Without hesitating, all three of the guardians raised their palms in a defensive stance and prepared for the assault. Again, the fire burst forth from Drelokh's mouth, cascading the three wizards in an intense inferno. The fires that once engulfed the guardians in the tunnels seemed to lack their devastating power.

The malice in the dragon's eyes grew even brighter. The sheer will and overall desire to destroy these wizards burned through his body and encompassed every fiber in his being. He had the opportunity to simply run, if he took flight now he could lay low in a safe haven and allow his body to recover. However, the dragon was too consumed in his desire to kill each of the guardians that all rationalization had left him. Pure adrenaline was now the driving force as he twisted his body, stumbling briefly on his wounded leg while swiping at the guardians with his powerful tail. Even in this weakened state there was little the three could do to avoid the attack as they couldn't jump or crouch to avoid the swing while their attempt at a defensive barrier was bashed away by the intense force.

Tristin and Keeris were both thrown into the rock wall of the cave, each receiving numerous minor contusions from the sharp scales along the dragon's tail. Darius, on the other hand, was a few paces closer to Drelokh as he attempted to talk him down from the battle and received a blow from the thicker, more muscular portion of the tail. Darius had no chance in defending the blunt force and was thrown in the arc of the tails swing, straight towards the opening of the cave. With no time to think, his natural instincts took over and he quickly pulled Heretius's dagger from his belt and sunk it into Drelokh's tail. Using the dagger as a handle, Darius hung on for dear life as he passed over the precipice of the caves opening and dangled a thousand feet above the rocky cliffs below.

Had the dragon known Darius was clinging to his tail he may have changed his tactics and cast him off into the abyss. However, with the numerous cuts across his body he could no longer feel the pain of his fatal wounds and therefore never noticed the small dagger that penetrated into his tail. Digging his talons into the rock Drelokh hurled his body headfirst at Tristin and Keeris attacking with his teeth. As the dragon bound towards them, the next few moments seemed to pass by in slow motion for the young guardians. Drelokh's eyes were pure black now, completely blinded by his hatred as he advanced, fire trickling from the sides of his mouth as he bared his teeth. The two also planted their feet and prepared to hold their ground. This was the final moment for the guardians, if they were unable to thwart this attack there would be no stopping the dragon's massive jaws from ending them. Keeris put all the might he had left behind his icy attack. This was the same frozen blast that he had used just hours prior on Audric, an attack that normally would have had little effect on a full-grown dragon. The cascading frozen stream of ice collided with the open jaws of Drelokh, dowsing the fires in this throat and caused him to defensively close his mouth. While this was happening, Tristin, wielding the sword he had taken from the fallen Audric, swung it in a full arc above his head and brought it down with all his might square on the dragon's head between his eyes. The powerful skull of Drelokh halted the fatal blow, yet still allowed the blade to sink a few inches into him.

The pain reeled through the red dragon's massive body as he raised himself up on his hind legs, screaming out with such an intense pain the guardians dropped to their knees and covered their ears. While chaotically thrashing around, Drelokh smashed his face and unfurled wings into the roof and side of the cave. With a deep tremor, large boulders began dislodging from the ceiling due to the dragon's frantic movements. Darius, who was able to let go of the dragon's tail after Drelokh rushed forward, pulled him back into the cave, and quickly cast a protection barrier above his companions to protect them from the falling rocks. As the massive stones fell, they repeatedly crashed with full force into Drelokh dropping him to the cave floor.

As the dust from the cave-in settled the three guardians looked out at the once mighty red dragon, now half entombed in stone. Cautiously, they advanced on Drelokh, uncertain if he still had the strength to continue his attack. With labored breathes the rock pile slowly rose and fell from the dragon's half collapsed lung.

"Listen, young warriors." As Darius made his way around the rubble, he stood with Keeris and Tristin near Drelokh's face, one of the few parts of his body that remained uncrushed from the fallen rocks. The blackness slowly melted from his eyes and was replaced by a dazzling turquoise. Momentarily, the three guardians were lost in the tranquility of Drelokh's eyes that seemed to swirl like an infinite galaxy in space.

Blood continued to stream down the dragon's face from the large cut he received from Tristin's new blade. "Please listen to me as I only have a few moments left." Drelokh coughed out blood as he struggled to continue talking. "Only now, at the end of all things, am I able to remember life before I let the malice take me. I wasn't always the harborer of evil in this world, there was a time when the guardians and I worked together." Drelokh tightened his face as the pain flooded through his body. "If Erquein survived his fall please tell him something for me. Let him know I'm sorry, and that the chalice of friendship, eroded by the blood of dragonstone can remain whole once more. He will understand." A small smile found its way to Drelokh's face as the brilliant turquoise color of his eyes again faded away, this time to a deep grey as the mighty red dragon took his final breath.

Chapter 27

Homecoming

Keeris quietly wiped tears from his eyes and the three guardians stood silently over the fallen body of their enemy. The joyful feeling that should have rushed forth after such an impossible victory now left a hollow and empty feeling in their hearts. It was true they had just saved the world from an unimaginable evil, yet with Drelokh's final breaths and repentance, they couldn't find it in them to celebrate his death.

After nearly an hour of silence in Drelokh's tomb, Darius spoke to his friends. "We may have won this battle, but there is still an immense enemy horde about to engage in combat with our friends and family at the bridge over the Vahnulth!"

Homecoming

"Darius is right!" Tristin quickly chimed in. "And this bridge won't hold back the enemy forces like before. We will never reach them in time but we need to let the other guardians know what happened here."

Darius' eyes grew wide as he frantically ran for the tunnel which they first traveled down. With a breath of relief, Darius found his pack near the mouth of the cave, untouched by the effects of the battle, and retrieved his Colifiate.

My fellow guardians, friends and comrades. The red dragon has been defeated! Tristin, Keeris and myself are all mostly unharmed and will be unable to reach you all and help with the upcoming battle on the Vahnulth. Please protect the people of Trubanius in our absence so we can all meet up again soon in celebration!

With that, Darius put his book back in his pack, slung it over his shoulders and put his arms around his friends as they began the long home march from Drelokh's tomb.

The following week passed by slowly and uneventfully for the three companions as they concluded their long journey. They had brief correspondences with the other guardians of the order and learned that the battle for the Vahnulth bridge at Tay's Crossing never took place. The unnatural death cry of Drelokh not only rang loud throughout the Shemod mountains, but was also heard all across Trubanius. This near mythological and legendary cry was ultimately what put an end to the war. After the armies of the red and black banner heard this ear-piercing scream, they instantly knew what it meant for their leader and what it would eventually mean for them. Without the tyrannical rule of the red dragon to command his forces, they were quickly disbanded and fled back to their dark corridors or to the reopened tunnels of Bhulek.

The three met no resistance in their travels, and their newfound abilities allowed them to travel with little fear of the unknown. After eight full days of cutting through the mountainous terrain and another full day of hiking through the forest, the two grimps and the kolerunt found themselves back in an all too familiar place for both Tristin and Keeris. They were now in the Misty Forest, the home of Keeris's people. The homecoming was a joyous one for the guardians as they were praised like kings amongst the kolerunts.

The time spent in the kolerunt village was

brief for Tristin and Darius. Although they were going to miss their friend as his absence from their group would leave an unfillable hole, deep in their hearts the grimps desperately wanted to return to the home they had left a lifetime ago. So, with tears shed, the three best friends said their farewells. They knew it would only be a temporary split, they not only had their books to keep in touch but also had plans to tour Trabanius and continue their growth as guardians soon enough. Yet for now, rest, relaxation and recovery were what they all needed.

The next two days were equally quiet as there wasn't much left for Darius and Tristin to say. They recounted their individual adventures while apart from one another as they finished the final leg of their adventure. Then, eight months after they had left the small confines of the grimp village they once again stepped foot back to the world where they grew up. The entire village had shown up to give the two a hero's welcome as both Darius and Tristin's parents ran towards their children and tackled them to the ground. Once the two were allowed to recompose themselves and come up for air another familiar face stood before them to greet his comrades. Heretius did what he could to hold the tears from his glazed eyes as he embraced both Tristin and Darius.

"My friends! If not for the accounts of all that had happened this year, I would have never guessed whom these two masters were that just walked into our small village! I couldn't be prouder of the incredible work and self-sacrifice you two have endured these many months. I have also never been this proud and honored to be known as a guardian! The company I now stand with could never in the history of our world be matched." At that Heretius could no longer hold back his emotions and for the first time in their lives the grimps watched as Heretius wept with his friends.

Slowly, Heretius was able to regain his composure as he addressed the rest of the village. "My friends, I know you all have your questions for our young hero's and there will soon be a massive banquet and festivities to follow. However, I need to ask you let both Darius and Tristin have but a short respite with me first. As you all know there is another in this village that would like to welcome our saviors as well!"

Both Darius and Tristin were slightly confused as Heretius ushered them from the village towards the clearing where Tristin had his first encounter with the fellowship of guardians. There, laying in the clearing was Erquein! A smile filled the dragon's face as he saw the grimps approach.

"Master Tristin, it has only been a few weeks since I left you in the swamps and yet you look as if you have fully shed your childish exterior and have downed yourself in the embodiment of a true warrior." Erquein then turned his gaze on Darius. "You must be Master Darius; I've heard many impressive stories of your adventures as well. I have lived countless years and have yet to meet the equal of the small band currently standing before me!"

Tristin ran to Erquein and threw his arms around the dragon's face. "We heard you fell! I thought Drelokh had killed you during your battle?"

Erquein turned his face into Tristin, nuzzling him slightly. "It is true that I was near moments from passing from this world. If not for the intervention from your order of guardians, I would never have escaped that torrent river. However, here I am! Worse for wear that is true enough, I will likely be unable to fly again till the summer. Drelokh definitely bested me in the battle, he was a fierce foe!"

Darius was standing by Tristin as he interrupted Erquein. "No, Drelokh didn't beat you! I would say at most the battle was a draw. When we came across the red dragon, he was nearly ready to collapse on the spot. Honestly, the three of us only barely managed to survive the encounter. Had you not fatally wounded him first I shudder to think of how Trubanius would look right now."

"Oh, that's right!" Tristin quickly pulled himself from Erquein so he could look the dragon in the eye. "When Drelokh was about to pass on, his eyes changed to a beautiful turquoise. It was then that he seemed to grieve what he had done and asked us to deliver an apology to you if you were still alive. He wanted us to tell you. *Let him know I'm sorry, and that the chalice of friendship, eroded by the blood of dragonstone can remain whole once more.* He said you would understand what that meant.

Briefly, Erquein's eyes shown with the same radiance that Drelokh's did before his death. "That is some incredible news my friends. I will try and explain what had happened in those moments. Firstly, I had once told both you, Tristin and Keeris, this as you flew on my back towards the swamps. A dragon is never truly good nor evil, we are simply beings that exist in this world. That is unless we forget ourselves in some way. It is much more complex than my simple explanation but what I'm trying to tell you is that, in those end moments of the red dragon's life, he once again became the dragon Drelokh that he once was. In those moments my brother returned to us, which warms my heart to no end! Now as to the second portion of my brothers' message, this is a mystery we had always guessed at, yet could never prove. That would be the mystery of "what" changed my brother from Drelokh to the red dragon and "why". You say he told you the *chalice of friendship*, that would be our brotherhood as dragons was eroded by the *blood of dragonstone*. Somewhere, now hidden within Trubanius or quite possibly Broudin at this moment, resides an incredible jewel. This gemstone is blood red in color and said to encase the heart of the first ever dragon. Whatever magic is housed in this stone is what ultimately turned my brother into the tyrant you knew him as."

There was a pause as the grimps took in the information that Erquein had just told them. Then Tristin looked to his friend and then back to the dragon. "So, are you telling us that there is a possibility that everything that has happened could happen again if this stone falls into the wrong hands? Or possibly even the right hands?"

Erquein tipped his head back and let out a powerful laugh. "You're right about one thing, master Heretius. These young proteges of yours will look for any excuse to keep on moving." The dragon then turned his attention back to Tristin and Darius. "The short answer to your question. I have no idea what the mysteries of the dragonstone hold. Your question could very well be true; however, it could just as simply be a pretty red rock cherished as the other gems of the world are."

Heretius put his arms on both the shoulders of Darius and Tristin. "That my friends is an adventure for another time. Today, we celebrate with the loved ones that are still with us! Let us revel in the victories this year has brought us. I can tell you there will always be mysteries this world has to offer, but those won't be solved tonight. Your families are waiting, they have waited for so long, let them be whole again!"

At that, the three grimps returned to the center of the village and joined in the festivities. The celebrations would last through the week as there was now so much for the entire village to be thankful for. The names of Darius, Tristin and Keeris would go down in grimp lore as the heroes that saved Trubanius. As the final rays of the sun sunk below the horizon on the final day of the celebration, so to concluded the last of days marked without an Age. For although the legend of the red dragon was now merely a memory, it was but a foothold for the Age to come.

~ *The Age of Vindication* ~

ABOUT THE AUTHOR

I've grown up and spent all of my life in a small town in central Wisconsin. I'm married to a beautiful wife and have been blessed with two fantastic children. I've spent the last 15 years working in a book bindery helping to bring the written words of others to life, now it's my turn.

Ever since being introduced to the world of creative writing by my 4th grade teacher, I was hooked. It's possible I was a bard in a past life. I love to tell stories, whether in written form or guiding adventurers through the fantasy realm of D&D. To witness someone react emotionally to a character that I've created brings so much joy and is a feeling that's hard to put into words. This book has been a labor of love that has taken nearly a lifetime to complete. Now that my first published novel is finished I can't wait to put pen to paper again and start weaving my next tale. I hope to see you again soon!